SIGNY'S MATES

A WOLF SHIFTER FATED MATES REVERSE HAREM ROMANCE

BILLIONAIRE WOLVES SERIES
BOOK FIVE

CHARMAINE LOUISE SHELTON

CONTENTS

Want FREE Books?   v
About Signy's Mates: A Wolf Shifter Fated Mates Reverse Harem Romance   vii

Chapter 1   1
Chapter 2   11
Chapter 3   19
Chapter 4   28
Chapter 5   37
Chapter 6   47
Chapter 7   57
Chapter 8   67
Chapter 9   78
Chapter 10   88
Chapter 11   102
Chapter 12   112
Chapter 13   125
Chapter 14   139
Chapter 15   148
Chapter 16   159
Chapter 17   170
Chapter 18   181
Chapter 19   198
Chapter 20   212
Preview Jagger The Temptation: A Wolf Shifter Fated Mates Paranormal Romance   223
Next in Series Signy Claimed: A Wolf Shifter Fated Mates Reverse Harem Romance   236

Want FREE Books?   239
Also By Charmaine Louise Shelton   241
About Charmaine Louise Shelton   245

WANT FREE BOOKS?

Want to know what happened to Jagger's best friend Dylan? Find out in *Dylan The Rogue: A Wolf Shifter Fated Mates Paranormal Romance* your FREE Book!

Click Cover Below or visit **bit.ly/ CLBooksDylanTheRogue** to subscribe to my newsletter for latest news and launches, books from my author friends, and sizzling reads in book promotions. Plus, start reading the steamy fated mates romance for bad boy wolf shifter Dylan.

ABOUT SIGNY'S MATES: A WOLF SHIFTER FATED MATES REVERSE HAREM ROMANCE

What happens when I suffer amnesia and three powerful wolf shifters rescue me from a plane crash?

I open my eyes and lose more than my precious mind to the gorgeous males of the Billionaire Wolves of New York. Snow bound and unrecognizable, they offer me shelter and time to heal. Even though I can't remember my past, my future promises just what I need to find love.

But Garrett, the pack leader, Dolph, his second, and Colin, the enforcer, share secrets with their special ops missions that put me in danger.

When they learn I'm Signy Larson the pack princess of Miami, they want to claim me as their fated mates queen and keep me in their fortress forever.

But will my family allow it? Better yet, will I?

*Their spicy reverse harem paranormal romance is a stand-alone trilogy in the sizzling **Billionaire Wolves Series** of inter-connecting stories featuring wolf shifter fated mates romance. Get a glimpse of their dynamism in other books.*

Anthem: "That's the Way Love Goes" Janet Jackson

https://www.youtube.com/watch?v=2b_KfAGiglc

Visit CharmaineLouiseBooks.com

CHAPTER 1

igny

THEY SAY the pampered life of a wolf shifter pack princess is all eyes on her and she gets what she wants. Loved and cherished by all. Her happiness reigns. Even more so when it's the Miami Wolves Pack. Actually, *Billionaire Wolves of Miami* as the other packs refer to us. With good reason, since we're the most powerful pack in the South.

Several millennia ago, Scandinavian Viking wolf shifters sailed from the Old World and landed along the East Coast of what's now the United States. The six packs headed by best friends who sought new lands moved throughout the continent to form territories, with ours settling here. The others govern Los Angeles, Sedona, Las Vegas, Aspen, and New York. We maintain close ties with our brethren through friendship, mating, and business. Plus, our Ruling Council gatherings keep us informed of happenings throughout the packs.

Sounds good, huh?

Well… Mine was a pretty sweet deal until our pack exploded with fated mates and newborn pups.

Not to say I'm anti-love and loathe little ones. Not at all.

It's just different, and I'm the odd one out.

Jagger Larson—my eldest brother at thirty to my twenty-six—took over from our father Marcus as the Alpha. Jagger is happy to allow me to continue as the pack princess, even though his and his fated mate High Witch Sage Waters' pup Tove is technically the new princess. But she's a youngster with no idea of what the position means. So, I'm more than pleased to maintain my status in the pack.

At twenty-eight, our brother Viggo reigns as the pack prince with Tove's fraternal twin Harald second. But Viggo also found his fated mate, human Maya Alejandra Perez Garcia, and settled down with their newborn pup Ulf recently. Even the self-proclaimed eternal pack playboy met his match.

Their best friends and consequently my big brothers— Tag Dahl, Rust Ingolf, and Dylan Vang—fell muzzle over paws for their fated mates, Wren Byrd, Natalie Moore, and Sasha Volkov, respectively. One after the other, they succumbed to the unique scents of their females—human and she-wolves. Soon after, more pups popped out.

Where does that leave me?

Here I sit on the deck of Jagger and Sage's Moon Island bayfront mansion as I bounce Inessa—Dylan and Sasha's pup—on my knees.

I glance around as we gather for dinner before the sun sets. The waters of Biscayne Bay glitter like diamonds around our pack's private island between South Beach on the barrier island and Edgewater on the coast. Laughter and conversations fill the tropical air. The constant breeze of the Atlantic Ocean lessens the humidity for a comfortable temperature. Its salty scent blends with the fragrance of the abundant jasmine and gardenia bushes. I inhale deeply and let my eyes drift close for a moment.

The images of my brothers and their females surrounded by their pups remain etched on the backs of my eyelids. Their outlines shimmer in the orange glow. All happy little families bonded by their love. I squeeze my lids and scrunch my nose to disperse the images.

A dull ache spreads across my chest, tugging at my heart. It clenches as the thoughts I attempt to ward off weave their way into my mind. Slowly, they move from the fringes.

Don't you want to find your fated mate?

Feel his love lift your spirit as it travels through your bond?

My breath catches, and I shake my head. But it's no use. The threads combine and wrap around my heart.

Oh, Signy, you know you ache for your other half.

You're older than your mother when she met your father.

Time is ticking...

Inessa's little hands cup my face as she giggles.

Thankful for the interruption, I open my eyes. Not now, Signy. Let it go. Leave your pity party for another time and enjoy your family.

Instead of dwelling on my lack of a mate, I zerbert the tip of Inessa's button nose. More giggles draw a smile on my face and push aside thoughts of loneliness.

"Siggy!"

She tries to say my name, and I laugh. She can't quite say it like the other little ones. Who can blame them? It's an old Scandinavian name meaning new victory. My parents named me after my mother Sigrid, or victory. Sweet, but not the easiest to say properly, even for adults.

With a grin, I lean in and zerbert Inessa's chubby cheeks.

She giggles and squirms to get down. Once on her feet, she scampers away, heading for the rest of the pups where they play on the other side of the deck. I watch them for a moment until a tug on my heart threatens to engulf me in loneliness again. Refusing to give in, I take a deep, cleansing breath and rise from the chaise lounge.

I don't need to worry about my fated mate. It's nearly impossible to find the one destined by the gods as your other half. The majority of wolf shifters bond with those they fall in love with or through an arranged mating. Some don't even believe in fated mates since the pairings prove rare. My brothers were beyond lucky.

So as much as I envy their kismet, I need to turn my focus on my goal of launching an online luxury boutique for curated pieces. Better to spend my time turning my love of fashion into a viable business and prove I can make my own way in life. Even though I'm the pack princess, I want my independence from my parents and my brothers. Who says I'll have time for a mate?

Sure thing, Signy.

Keep telling yourself that.

I scowl at the unwanted internal dialogue.

"Hey, Signy. Are you all right?"

Pulled from my musings, my gaze turns to Sage. Her emerald green eyes move from my ice blue ones to scan my face. Even though her magick allows her to read people's minds, she doesn't, unless it's necessary. And I'm thankful since I'd rather no one knows the depths of my loneliness. I don't want to lessen their happiness with feelings of pity for me. I couldn't deal with the sympathetic looks, even though they would mean well.

I plaster a smile on my face and nod.

"Of course! I'm just thinking Viggo better not burn the steaks. I'm starved!"

I loop my arm through hers and move us towards the outdoor kitchen. In my periphery, I notice Sage eyes me. But I keep the smile on my face and babble on about how delicious dinner smells. A frown mars her flawless toffee complexion as she nods.

"If you say so. But if you want to share what's truly on your mind, I'm here for you as your sister or your pack Luna. Whichever you need. Okay?"

A lump rises in my throat. I can only nod, afraid the sudden tears will clog my voice if I speak.

Sage squeezes my arm.

"Good. We're a family. And family comes above all."

The loneliness recedes as the tendrils constricting my heart loosen. I may not have my mate—fated or otherwise. But I have my family that loves me unconditionally, and I will give up everything for them.

As though sensing my thoughts, Viggo lifts his head. Eyes the same as mine focus on me. They sparkle as a grin spreads across his handsome face and the breeze ruffles his fiery copper red hair.

"Just in time, my lovely sisters! Grab a plate. Dinner is served."

My stomach rumbles its gratitude, and we laugh.

Settled at the oval teak table between Natalie and Wren, the conversation flows. I lose myself in the banter over the Miami Heat basketball game between my brothers and the plans for a Girls' Night Out.

But their conversation stops when they hear Sasha giggle about me getting my groove on finally. Their lull draws our attention, and our laughter tapers to silence. Their eyes drill me. My cheeks heat from the intensity and knowing what's coming.

Naturally, Jagger speaks up first.

"And how exactly might my baby sister get her 'groove on' and with whom?"

Viggo nods and cocks an eyebrow.

Sasha glances at me.

I shake my head, accustomed to their overprotective behavior. Ever since I hit my teens, they've successfully blocked any male from dating me. The only time I truly appreciated their interference was when our father arranged for me to mate an Alpha who was much older than me. My father wanted to form an alliance with the other pack, and I was the conduit.

Viggo found me crying on the other side of Moon Island and called Jagger. Although our father was pack Alpha, Jagger convinced him the match wasn't fair to me. Thankfully, our father relented. But since then, my brothers make it their mission to vet any male who so much as glances in my direction. If he breathes wrong, they pounce and scare him away.

Yeah, another aspect of being the pack princess? I'm untouchable. Loved, cherished, and guarded.

No wonder I'm still a virgin at my age.

Sage—the only one who doesn't shrink under Jagger's Alpha dominance—quirks an perfectly arched eyebrow.

"Oh, Jagger, don't you think it's time Signy finds her fated mate? Like you and the others?"

He growls and shakes his head.

"We haven't found a suitable male wolf for Signy."

"What about the Alpha from—"

"No."

"The one from—"

"No."

"What's wrong with the cute beta—"

"Hell, no!"

Sage throws her hands up. Natalie rolls her eyes. Sasha bites her lip. Maya sighs.

I sit back and fold my arms over my chest. I'll never overcome the loneliness if my brothers don't let up enough for me to meet someone. Before I can voice just that, Wren speaks up.

"Well, how do you expect Signy to find her fated mate if you overbearing big brothers block her at every chance?" Wren asks as she pins her gaze on each of them in turn. Gold flecks spark in the mink brown as her wolf hovers below the surface. "Don't you think you're being a bit much?"

Tag cocks his head at her. Still new to wolf pack dynamics, Wren doesn't realize the challenge in her tone of voice and in her eyes. However, our pack beta is quick to remind her.

"Careful, my love. We are in an informal family setting. But you must watch your tone when you address our Alpha. Understood?"

She purses her lips but nods, then verbally responds when Tag raises his eyebrow.

I, on the other hand, can stand no more.

"Jagger, I appreciate you and the others watching out for me. But I am a grown she-wolf and can make decisions of my own," I say, then continue despite his growl. "I'm not saying I'm going to jump into bed with every male I see. But if I so choose, I will have more than one date with the same guy. With no interference from any of you. Can you agree to let me live my love life? I'm asking you as my brother."

He studies my face. Ice blue eyes glint silver with his dominant silvery white wolf.

My black wolf whines under the intense gaze of our Alpha. She wants to drop to the ground and bare her belly and neck in submission. However, I return his stare as his sister and won't back down. I need him to respect my wishes. His behavior reminds me to seek my independence pronto.

Jagger must sense my determination. His wolf recedes, and his eyes return to their regular color. He glances at Viggo, Tag, Rust, and Dylan. I watch as they communicate silently. Jagger shifts in his seat to look at me.

I search his face for any clue of his decision. Finding none, my heart thuds against my ribs. The pulse roars in my ears. It almost drowns out his words.

"Signy, we want what is best for you. Our intentions are not to prevent you from finding your true love. They are to protect you from those who would dare to use you for their gain. You know the importance of our pack above all others. We will not allow you to be a pawn in some male's scheme and will destroy anyone who hurts you."

He pauses as his wolf resurfaces at the mention of harm to me. The others voice their growly agreement. I shudder, knowing they mean every word. The gods help any male who steps wrong.

"However, we know the joy of finding our fated mates

and want the same for you. I agree your love life is your own and you should live it—"

I sag in relief and dispel the air I didn't realize I was holding. A grin spreads across my face. But it stops halfway as Jagger continues.

"However, I will approve before a male wolf claims you. Nonnegotiable. I speak as your brother and as your Alpha. Do you understand?"

Before he can change his mind, I agree wholeheartedly.

Why would it be an issue?

CHAPTER 2

arrett

"FIRE IN THE HOLE!"

I duck my head at my pack's head enforcer Colin Voll's warning as it comes through our ear comms. He crouches near the reinforced steel double doors of a warehouse a few feet ahead of the team. The explosives he set on the doors and on a pair in the back will dismantle the locks and allow us entry. Then we'll take out the fuckers who kidnapped the she-wolves.

Not long ago, I partnered with Dylan Vang—a member of the Miami Wolves Pack—when wolf shifters from Russia captured his fated mate Sasha Volkov for the second time. They brought her and others from her village across the globe to Pennsylvania. She was fortunate to escape to New York City, where she met Dylan. But they found her with the help of one of my trusted men and returned her to the clutches of Kirill Gusev. We ended both of them. However, that was just a peek inside the dark underground cells of kidnapped she-wolves.

A worldwide racket centers on male wolf shifters raiding remote packs to take unclaimed she-wolves of breeding age. They keep them bound with silver handcuffs or chains to prevent them from escaping. The silver bites into their flesh and burns. The males force the she-wolves to breed with them, then sell the pups on the underground market. Many packs lack females, so the value of she-wolf pups is higher. Desperate Alphas will do anything to increase their packs' numbers.

And all this shit happens right under my nose. I—the mighty Alpha of the New York Wolves Pack who controls the North—had no idea until Vang approached me.

What makes it worse is I'm a decorated Captain in the U.S. Army and to top it all off a Green Beret. A don't fuck with me Green Beret. And these fuckers messed with the wrong wolf shifter. Now they're on my radar, I will elimi-nate each and every one of their sorry asses.

And my A-Team is up to the task.

Not only is Colin my pack enforcer, he's a First Lieu-tenant and my A-Team Weapons Sergeant. I rounded out my team with First Lieutenant Dolph Pihl—my pack beta and A-Team Intelligence and Operations Sergeant—and trained pack members. As their Commanding Officer, I made it our mission to eliminate the racket one nest at a time.

Inseparable since pups twenty-nine years ago, I chose Dolph and Colin to fight beside me on this mission, just as I did during our Special Forces days. We graduated from the United States Military Academy as Second Lieutenants and rose in the ranks. We followed our fathers and theirs before them to West Point and in our roles in the pack.

The three of us became guerrilla warfare experts and use unconventional tactics to fight terrorists abroad. No longer on active duty—although we're called in for special missions—we focus those skills to dismantle the racket. That is when we're not running Moen, Inc.—my family's multibillion-dollar arms and aircraft manufacturing company based in New York City. Thanks to it, we have the latest weapons and transportation for our missions.

This latest ring operates in a remote area of northern Maine across the Canadian border opposite Edmundston. A tip came in after a local vet made the news for video footage of a naked female running through the facility and out onto the street during the night. Since the town has less than two hundred people, they don't have street cameras. They lost sight of the female, and she disappeared.

But it was enough to warrant an investigation by Dolph. He used his intelligence skills to track down the cell. I sent a small tactical unit to monitor activity for a few days. Their intel provided enough details for us to plan this mission. Now, we carry it out.

"All clear!"

Colin's declaration increases my heart rate as adrenaline rushes through my body. Enhanced vision and hearing sharpen. Fingers flex on my Moen semi-automatic weapon. My skin prickles.

In my mind's eye, my massive jet black wolf strikes the ground with his sizable paws eager for the fight. His glacial blue eyes flash electric blue as he stares back at mine. We nod in unison. I raise my hand for the signal to move ahead. We're full-on commando.

I split my team into two groups to approach from opposite sides with the warehouse in the middle. Some of them will shift into wolves while the others remain in human form with semi-automatic weapons, handguns, and knives. A group will free the she-wolves and get them to the helicopters and medics we left a distance away.

When we arrived, we eliminated the kidnappers patrolling the area. As we pass, I see their throats slit from ear to ear and eyes poked out. The clean-up crew will handle them.

"Got your back, Alpha."

"As always, Dolph."

We emerge from the thick forest that surrounds the site on all sides provides ample coverage. In clusters, we move fast while keeping low. Shouts in French from the warehouse indicate we surprised the male wolf shifters as expected. Since French is one of the seven languages I speak, I easily understand their calls to fight to the death. And to the death they will go.

Pitiful cries from the she-wolves reach my ears.

I growl and lunge forward to flatten my back against the outer wall. Thick white smoke billows from the blasted area after a team member extinguished the fire to clear our entry. Unimpeded since we wear protective goggles and masks, we enter.

Snarls come from our left, then three massive wolves appear. They snap their jaws, ears flattened to their heads, and hackles raised. One by one, they leap into the air, claws extended.

Pow. Pow. Pow.

The wolves crash to the ground, writhing as they howl in agony. Silver-dipped ammo finishes them. But we have no time to gloat. More approach, along with those in human form armed with rifles. We exchange gunfire as we work our way through the vast space. We use containers stacked high as shields.

I don't care the foot soldiers get killed. I want their leader Raulf Blaise and his second Gilles Bernard. My eyes search for the interior office where heat signatures indicate four figures. I spot it ahead and give the code word for Dolph and Colin to follow. They confirm and we rush towards the office.

As we near, the heat signatures disappear one by one.

Dolph must notice since he turns to me with a scowl. I signal to move in. Colin takes point with Dolph in the rear. The door gives way to Colin's swift kick. It bangs against the wall. He growls as his eyes focus on the middle of the office, where a trapdoor stands open.

We approach the gaping hole in the floor with caution. Darkness greets us. But it's no deterrent, as our wolf eyesight provides a clear view of a mounted ladder leading to a dirt floor. The fuckers built an escape route.

Colin glances at me, and I nod. He drops through the hole into a defensive crouch, semi-automatic raised.

"All clear. Tunnel," he says into the mouthpiece as he steps forward to free space for us to jump down.

Dolph and I follow. Immediately, we charge ahead.

Steel beams reinforce the dirt ceiling and walls. Paw prints mix with boot marks on the dirt-packed floor. The numbers indicate frequent use. Here and there, single bare bulbs glow dimly in the darkness. It's silent until we round a bend and come face-to-face with two giant wolves. Their growls echo around us.

Without breaking stride, Colin and I pop them in the chest. They drop. We race on.

Chuff., Chuff. Chuff.

The distinctive sound of a helicopter's whirling rotors fills the air. The force of the rotor downwash whips up the dirt floor, obscuring our vision.

I growl, pissed Blaise and Bernard may slip away. An extra burst of speed gets us up the incline to the opening of the tunnel. Colin raises his semi-automatic for the shot.

"Stand down! I want them alive!"

He lowers the rifle.

Blaise peers down at us. A feral grin spreads across his face. My eyes lock on his as I bare my extended fangs. He throws his head back and howls. I clench my jaw as the triumphant sound rises above the rotors.

To fuck with him, I shoot a round just wide of the tail end.

His howl stops abruptly as he swings around to check for damage. When he faces me again, I point two clawed fingers at my eyes, then turn them towards him. He mimics my move as Bernard banks the helicopter towards the Canadian border.

"Motherfuckers!"

Colin kicks the camouflage tarp they used to hide the helicopter.

"Dammit. The intel didn't include the tunnel or the helo," Dolph adds as he watches it disappear into the distance.

"Make up for it by tracking their whereabouts," I say as I clap them on the shoulders. "This is far from over, boys. For now, we handle this situation."

We run through the tunnel and reemerge in the warehouse. A quick glance confirms an enforcer's announcement over the ear comm that they secured the building and the she-wolves arrived at our helicopters. As we pass through, I connect with my team through the telepathic bond I share with pack members as they're Alpha.

Fortunately, we only sustain a few injuries. They'll recover thanks to our enhanced healing ability. Those who are mobile move out for the helicopters, while others get help.

"Alpha, we caught this sneaky one hiding in a container and confiscated his laptops."

Now, a feral grin spreads across my face as I stare at a slight male wolf shifter. His eyes widen in fear at the sight of my toothy grin. It doesn't take a rocket scientist to realize he must be Blaise's tech guru.

"Well done. He'll ride with me. Put a hood over his head. We're taking him to The Fortress."

CHAPTER 3

Signy

"WELL, I LOVE YOUR IDEA!"

"How perfect for you!"

"Your selections for my mate bonding ceremony dress were ah-mazing! You're a natural, Signy."

"Even the maternity outfits you picked out were fabulous. I didn't feel like I was wearing a tent!"

"Your sense of style rivals spreads in *Vogue* any day."

I grin as my girls react to my news about the online boutique—Signy's Secret Cache.

With me being MIA, over the last few weeks, they insisted I make good on my promise for a Girls' Night Out. Naturally, we choose Club Hati since it's one of Larson Enterprises, Inc.'s properties and a spot for wolf shifters and humans to mingle on the dance floor. Plus, it's one of the few places my brothers allow me to frequent without my bodyguard Tomas. Our pack enforcers serve as security and will handle any situations that may impact my wellbeing. Sigh. Before I got my groove on, I shared the news with my girls.

I set my thoughts of a mate aside to delve into my independence move. I met with advisors and created the business plan. Then arranged trips to the fashion capitals of the world to find pieces for my collection. First up New York for Fashion Week.

My grin widens as I respond, "Thank you so much! I'm plenty nervous. But this is what I want to do. I haven't told my parents or brothers yet. First, I want to get the ball rolling and solidify all the moving parts. So, I'd appreciate it if you don't mention my plan to them."

They agree wholeheartedly with zipped lips and crossed hearts. I giggle at their dramatic responses, and they join in. Once we settle down, I tell them about my next step to fly to New York in the morning and make another request.

"I only told my parents and brothers I'm going for Fashion Week as usual, not the additional reason. So, lips sealed."

Sage squeals and stands with her glass of mojito raised.

"Here's to Signy's new venture. May she have much success in all her endeavors—"

"And get out from underneath her brothers' thumbs!" Wren cuts in with a smirk.

We clink glasses and sip our cocktails.

"Now, let's get this party started! I didn't wear this cute little number despite Viggo's protests for nothing, ladies!"

Maya exclaims as she stands and shimmies in her silver lamé mini dress. The lights sparkle on it as her hips move to the sensuous beat of the music.

I nod and jump to my feet, looping arms with her as we head to the dance floor. My heart swells with happiness. Soon I'll be completely free!

"Good morning, Signy."

I smile at the flight attendant and return her greeting as I board my Gulfstream G650 private jet at Miami International Airport.

"The pilot and co-pilot confirm we're ready for takeoff once you arrive. Would you care for something to drink or eat before we take to the air, or would you prefer to wait until we level off?"

"I'm good. Kindly tell them to take off. Thank you."

Her eyes flick to Tomas as he enters behind me before she nods and closes the jet's passenger door and heads to the cockpit.

I walk down the aisle of the spacious jet. It's comprised of areas with plush white leather chair groupings, a sofa opposite a silver lacquer console with a flat-screen televi-sion above, and a bedroom with a bathroom in the rear. I settle on a chair and drop my handbag on the one next to me and secure my seatbelt.

"Welcome aboard, Signy. We'll make it to JFK in just under three hours. I'll let you know when you're free to move about the cabin."

I nod even though he can't see me and glance over my shoulder at Tomas, who chose the sofa as his spot. Of course, he's with me for the trip. Jagger would never let me travel as far as New York without my bodyguard. I sigh and turn my gaze to the window.

After the pilot gives the all-clear, I release my seatbelt and reach for my laptop. Might as well review my schedule for the shows and meetings. The flight attendant serves breakfast and chats with Tomas. I grin as they flirt with one another.

Wolf shifters are sexual creatures and view intimacy as any other necessity in life. Unlike humans, we have no hang-ups about sex or nudity. Even though I'm a virgin, I'm very familiar with my pussy and what makes my toes curl thanks to my faithful B.O.B. I grin, knowing it's stowed in my luggage. Always ready for use!

My thoughts shift from my pleasure to Tomas and the flight attendant. My enhanced hearing picks up their plan for a hook up later tonight, presumably after I'm tucked in my suite. I wouldn't put it past Tomas to bolt the door shut or to set an alarm on it. I shake my head and swipe through my TikTok FYP.

An hour later, turbulence hits the jet. The co-pilot informs us of a change in the weather and to buckle up. My eyes move to the window. Gray mixes with the white fluffy clouds and snowflakes land on the glass.

"Okay, Signy. Your seatbelt's secure?"

I glance up to find Tomas standing in the aisle. His eyebrows meet over concern-filled brown eyes. They flick to my lap, and he nods.

"Buckle up before I sit down."

I let the command in his voice go and do as directed, just as the jet drops a few inches. He mutters a curse and returns to the sofa. My gaze returns to the window.

In minutes, the visibility lessens. Snow swirls around the jet, enveloping us in a white cocoon. It would be lovely if the jet wasn't dipping with the turbulence. Breakfast threatens to reappear as my stomach drops. I swallow and lower the shade as I turn away from the window. My eyes close as I take a deep, cleansing breath. They pop open when I hear movement in the aisle.

The flight attendant hovers with wide eyes.

"Do you mind if I sit here with you? I'd rather not sit alone in the crew area."

"Of course. I don't blame you."

She smiles gratefully and sits across from me.

"I love to fly. But I hate bad weather," she says with a fear in her voice.

"Tell me about it."

We sit in silence as the pilot and co-pilot maneuver the jet. Then all hell breaks loose.

"An unexpected blizzard swept in from the Atlantic Ocean as we fly near New York! Stay seated while we change route to avoid the worse of it," the pilot announces.

Unfortunately, the change does little to keep the jet out of the storm. It jounces in the violent turbulence. Needing to see what's happening, I raise the window's shade.

When I last glanced out the window, only thick swirls of snow appeared. The white fluffy clouds replaced by ominous gray ones until nothing was visible. I could see not even the wing or its flashing light.

I throw myself back against the plush leather seat and tighten my seatbelt. I reach for my mobile in the seat next to me. But the jet drops. The mobile flies from the seat and skitters across the floor. I cry out in horror as it crashes against the wall. The cracking of the screen lets me know I have no means of calling for help. I can't reach my parents or my brothers in Miami. Nor anyone else in our pack. My wolf whines in despair.

The pilot announces they're going to circumvent the storm and reroute from the flight plan to JFK. The monitors show a chance to avoid the worse of the storm if they fly further north of New York City.

Tomas calls for me to remain calm and buckled tight. I whimper in response as the turbulence worsens. Gods, help us!

"Keep your head down and hold on, Signy! Hold on! Oh, gods—"

The flight attendant shouts from her seat while the pilot and co-pilot attempt to regain control of the jet.

Now, I wonder if anything would have made a difference as the jet banks left and drops several feet. The change in course is so severe, bile rises in my throat. I choke it down as I hold my head between my knees. Tears stream down my cheeks as I sob.

As a young she-wolf, I can survive most damage with my enhanced healing. Only silver can inflict fatal harm. But this? Flying miles up in the sky during a freak snowstorm that blocks visibility for the pilot and co-pilot? Not an easily recoverable situation should we crash.

My heart clenches at the thought. Please gods, no!

How can I go from poring over the latest edition of *Vogue* while listening to my favorite playlist to begging for my life? All I wanted was to go to New York Fashion Week as I do every season and start my online boutique with finds from the shows. Now, I wish I'd stayed at home.

All thoughts blow from my mind as the front of the jet dips. The seatbelt digs into my pelvis as I hang from the seat. My waist-length black hair covers my face like a curtain. A scream rips from my throat. It blends with the flight attendant's wail. Tomas shouts curses.

"We're going down! Brace yourselves!"

The pilot's terrified shouts make my blood run cold.

My ears pop as I scream. My hands reach out but flail with nothing to hold.

The jet jerks up enough for me to sit back with a gasp as my body pulls away from the seatbelt. I swipe my hair out of my eyes and swivel my head. The interior of the jet is a mess.

"Oh, fuck!"

The pilot curses as something drags along the bottom of the jet. Metal screeches, lights flicker, alarms sound. Cold air fills the cabin. Tendrils of smoke follow.

We have no time to react as the jet plummets.

The flight attendant and I stare in stark fear at one another.

My wolf throws herself to the ground. She reminds me to brace myself for impact. Arms lift to the sides of my head as I lower my chest to my knees. Fingers intertwine. I say a silent pray.

Then boom…

Cold. So very cold.

My trembling body wakes me. Every inch screams in pain. I black out.

"—way. Over here!"

"Holy shit! This is the worse crash I've ever seen. And that's saying something."

"Where's the rest of it? Fuck…"

"Check her pulse. Is she breathing?"

Calloused fingers wrap around my wrist. Gently, they skim across the delicate skin. A jolt of electricity zips from the touch and up my arm. I cry out.

"She's alive!"

"Thank the gods."

"What about the others?"

Others? No! Please let them be alive, too.

Another jolt—but not a pleasurable one—courses through me as I try to sit up.

"Do not move."

Something warm infused with the enticing scents of sandalwood and vanilla covers me. Stubble scratches my neck. A deep inhalation against my skin makes me shudder. I cry out in a combination of ecstasy and agony. The man hisses. He jerks away.

"No, fucking way," he mutters.

"Do you smell that?"

"She can't be."

Who are these men?

My eyelids hurt as they flutter open. Blurry images in the shapes of three enormous men appear in the darkness. I blink to clear my vision, then reopen my eyes.

Glacial blue ones stare down at me. I watch mesmerized as they darken to cobalt, then flash electric blue.

The other two men snarl and growl. Surprised, my gaze shifts to them.

But a rumble draws my attention to the first man's face.

The air leaves my lungs as my mouth falls slack.

Jet black hair frames chiseled cheekbones and firm jaw. The silky strands hang to his bulging pecs. Muscular arms fold across his broad chest, covered in only a white tank top. On top of it, black dog tags hang from a black chain-link and leather necklace. My gaze follows the chain up to his magnificent face.

He studies me with an intensity that makes me tremble, and not from the cold.

Then darkness descends once again.

CHAPTER 4

olph

"*She can't be.*"

Fuck me.

I stagger where I stand as my knees buckle at one intoxicating whiff. I close my eyes and inhale deeply.

A spark ignites. It blazes a trail, firing along every fiber of my being. Then it explodes at the base of my cock. Instantly, it thickens and lengthens along my thigh. A pearl of pre-cum beads at the bulbous tip. My cock throbs with need. A lust-laced growl slips past my lips like an erotic prayer to the gods, offering thanks for my fated mate.

The unique scent of the she-wolf whose scent I was born imprinted on my soul entices me like no other. The forest after a spring rain, woody and earthy with a hint of wild honey straight from the comb. My breath goes out in a rush. Eagerly, I inhale again. Another carnal wave washes over me.

Mine!

Possessiveness like I've never known emerges from my depths. It churns in my gut and grips my heart. My fingers flex before they curl into fists. A snarl rips from my chest as Garrett crouches next to the severely injured she-wolf. His only reaction to my snarl is his hands fisting on his thighs. However, his gaze never strays from her face.

Even battered and bruised, she captivates us.

Although tangled with bits of detritus, her waist-length hair shines like polished ebony. It frames her heart-shaped face with a few strands stuck against the bloody cuts on her otherwise smooth skin. Despite the paleness of her complexion, it hints at a sun-kissed tone. Her Cupid's bow lips marred by a deep gash undoubtedly caused by her teeth biting into the soft flesh during the impact. Based on the length of her sprawled and twisted body, I guess her height a foot less than my six feet, eight inches. She's a young and healthy she-wolf.

For a brief moment, her eyes flutter open. The stunning ice blue orbs flick from Garrett to settle on Colin and me as we snarl and growl like feral beasts. But the selfish bastard rumbles to draw her attention back to him.

Jealousy rips through me as I watch her react to him on a carnal level—a soft gasp, swollen lips part, body shudders. Then her eyes close. The spell breaks.

My breath expels on a low growl.

I've heard the tales of a male wolf shifters' first encounters with their fated mates. Their mystical reactions to the she-wolves' the stuff of romance novels read by females. At least that was what I thought. Now, I'm not so sure they're fairy tales.

Sure, I believe my other half exists—somewhere in the world. And I've been all over the globe with not so much as a hint of her unique scent. Fucked plenty of she-wolves and human females. But none ever struck me to my core as this she-wolf who fell from the sky right in our pack's territory. A true fairy tale to tell my pups. Go figure.

Add to it the urge to fight Garrett—and Colin, for that matter, whose growls prove he's just as taken by her as we are—and I'm losing my shit. Never have I wanted to physically attack my best friends, especially over a female. We've shared too many to be bothered by possessiveness and jealousy. But the green-eyed monster takes over my senses even as my giant golden wolf prowls in my periphery. Gold sparks in his topaz eyes as he watches the scene before him.

He recognizes the she-wolf as his mate and wants to mark and to claim her. Now. No matter who he has to tear apart to make her his. And I agree.

Garrett rises. His eyes linger on the she-wolf before he turns his electric blue gaze to Colin and me. His wolf is close to the surface, as are ours. No doubt he is eager to lay claim to her.

I snarl at the thought.

His eyes narrow on me.

"I have an idea of what's going on here," he says as his eyes flick between Colin and me. He puts his Alpha command behind his next words. "However, we do not have time for squabbles. Colin, secure the area. Dolph, radio to the others to help bury the dead after you take photos of them. Keep an eye out for identifications. We need all the information we can get to learn who they are. I'll get the she-wolf to The Fortress where the medic can exam her. I'm concerned she's not healing."

My wolf grumbles, and Colin shakes his head.

Garrett cocks an eyebrow as his features harden.

"Understood?"

"Yes, Alpha," we respond in unison begrudgingly.

He eyes us until we lower our gazes out of respect for him as pack Alpha.

When he pivots, I watch as he scoops the she-wolf into his arms. Mine ache to hold her as a pained moan slips past her lips. He cradles her to his broad chest. Worry softens his features. His eyes linger on her face until she settles with a sigh. His lips brush her forehead.

Jealousy sparks anew.

It's on the tip of my tongue to demand he keeps his mouth off her and I take her to safety. But Garrett strides past me, headed towards the snowmobiles. I turn and watch as the blizzard blocks them from view. Loss creates a hollow in my chest. Unconsciously, my fist presses against the ache.

"Let's get this shit wrapped up already. What a fucking disaster."

Colin's words interrupt my thoughts. He stomps off in the opposite direction.

I scrub a hand over my face and pull out my radio.

Might as well make this a quick as possible so I can get back to The Fortress and to *my* mate.

~

COLIN

"DO YOU SMELL THAT?"

What the hell is it, and why did my knees damn near fold underneath me???

My wolf's growl fills the air. His amber eyes flash gold as his massive tawny body paces on the fringes of my mind's eye. Powerful muscles ripple beneath his fur.

What's got his hackles raised?

I glance at Dolph, wondering if he smells the woody and earthy scent of the forest after a spring rain with a dash of floral honey dripping from the comb. Something must get him.

His eyes widen and narrow as his fists clench and a snarl pours from his mouth. He's as agitated as my wolf. And me, if I'm honest.

But why???

I follow his line of sight to the she-wolf on the ground, where Garret hovers over her. For some reason, the image of her draped in his jacket further pisses off my wolf. A deep growl resonates in my chest.

Shocked, I shake my head to clear it of the inexplicable anger thrumming through my tense body. I scent the air to determine the source of the intoxicating fragrance. Despite we're in the middle of a blizzard, I detect it emanates from the prone she-wolf.

Her perfume?

With no patience for the mystery, I shake my head again as Garrett stands. He casts a lingering look at the she-wolf, whose eyes closed. I wonder at his protective stance over her, then flick my gaze to Dolph. His stormy topaz eyes zone in on the female. These two act as though they've never seen a she-wolf before. I'm pissed I must be missing something. Whatever.

Dolph's snarl brings my gaze back to him. Before I can ask what the hell is going on, Garrett adds to the mystery, proclaiming he knows. At least that makes one of us since I'm clueless as fuck. Unfortunately, I have no time to ask for specifics since he barks orders before he carries the she-wolf away. I shake my head once more.

As I watch them disappear into the swirling snow and darkness, my heart clenches. Unease fills my chest with a sense of loss. I ignore the odd sensation. However, my wolf throws his head back for a mournful howl. It ignites a determination to get back to The Fortress with a quickness.

"Let's get this shit wrapped up already. What a fucking disaster."

Without another glance at Dolph, I head to the wreckage. Since the private jet crashed within our pack's territory, it's up to us to handle the situation. No human involvement allowed.

Millennia ago, our pack settled on the twelve-mile long and four-mile wide island in what's now known as the Atlantic Ocean off the shore of East Hampton, New York. The perfect location for wolf shifters to live amongst humans in plain sight. Well, not so plain as they can't see the full extent of our private island set in its own bay because of the dense foliage. Moen Island serves as our base, with most of the families and singles living on it, while others reside in nearby Manhattan.

Because the New York Wolves Pack runs the North, our full territory extends beyond the city and well beyond the state's borders. Our territory abuts the Miami Wolves Pack to the South and the Aspen Wolves Pack to the West.

Fortunately for the she-wolf and the others who crashed, our territory is so vast. If Garret, Dolph, and I weren't at The Fortress in Upstate New York, the surviving she-wolf would have perished along with the others. In just the brief time I saw her, I could tell the injuries she sustained are massive. Hell, if she weren't a wolf shifter, she would be dead. The others were not as lucky. But we'll give them proper burials and inform their loved ones.

At the thought of losing the female, a band constricts around my heart. A gasp escapes my mouth at the unexpected reaction. Unconsciously, a hand rises to rub circles on the painful spot. When I realize, I shake my head and clench my fist.

What the fuck?

"Damn, what a messed-up situation."

"And a she-wolf survived all this? She must be something special—"

A possessive growl rumbles across the radio before Dolph responds to the others from our team.

"Yeah, let's get this done with a quickness."

Still confused by his earlier behavior and this reaction, I shake my head again as I tromp around the wreckage. Hell, I thought I was the prickliest bastard of the three of us— the supreme alphahole. Something has the level-headed one on edge. When we finish with this situation, I'll have answers.

The jet's fuselage broke and scattered as it descended. The wings and tail clipped and the engines detached along the jet's path. Following the trail, the wreck cut large swaths in the surrounding forest. Fires char the areas. Fortunately, the freak blizzard blasting snow and sleet contains the fires to the vicinity, avoiding further damage. In time, the storm will smother the fires.

For now, I check the area as best I can, given the limited visibility, even with my enhanced vision. The snow already covers the area in a thick blanket with no luggage or other identifying details in sight.

Who the hell can they be? Certainly not any of our wolf shifters, as we would have recognized their scents. Perhaps they were flying over New York and heading to Canada or out West.

I move quickly as the ache in my chest builds. Dolph's short patience barked over the radio spurs me on to complete the task as eager to return to The Fortress as he.

"Colin. We're done and heading back."

I snarl at Dolph's announcement over the radio as the roar of his snowmobile's engine follows. He doesn't wait for my response and clicks off. My head swings left and right for one last check of the wreckage site. With no more I can do given the weather, I give in to my wolf's demand and race towards my snowmobile.

Yeah, I'll get my answers as soon as we return to The Fortress. And they better not piss me off.

CHAPTER 5

arrett

I CAN BARELY CONTROL my wolf as he gnashes his teeth and paces. His nostrils flare—as do mine—to capture the tantalizing scent of the forest after a spring rain, woody and earthy with a hint of wild honey straight from the comb. The scent of this fragile she-wolf in my arms swirls around me, wrapping me in a cocoon of her deliciousness.

But the unique scent of my fated mate isn't the only smell my wolf and I detect that sets us on edge. The coopery tang of her blood and the sharp sting of her pain mix with her natural aroma. The fact our mate is hurt drives us feral. I barely contained myself at the recognition of who she is to us. And what baffles me are Dolph and Colin's reactions to her.

Their possessive growls and snarls at me being near and holding her surprised me. They can't possibly believe she's their fated mates. Not when she's mine. Mine!

A whimper at my growl draws my attention to her as I trudge through snowdrifts as high as my thighs, headed for the snowmobile. My enhanced hearing allows me to hear her cry above the roar of the wind gusts. I glance down at her battered face.

Her eyebrows knit together as another pitiful moan slips past her parted lips. Long lashes cast shadows on her swollen cheeks. Eyelids scrunch. She cries out as a violent shudder racks her ravaged body.

Instinctively, a rumble rises from the depths of my chest to soothe her distress. The vibrations reverberate around her as I increase the pressure of my arms at her shoulders and beneath her knees. I bring her closer to my chest, careful not to squeeze too tight and cause further damage to her.

My wolf whimpers as he detects our mate's pain. His eyes flash electric blue with concern for her wellbeing. My skin itches with his need to burst free to protect her.

I shake my head and push him back, needing to remain in my human form as the best means to help her now.

"Don't worry, little one. I will always keep you safe," I murmur against her hair. Then I frown.

How the hell can I always keep her safe when missions put me in danger each time?

And the main ones we're dealing with involve rings that kidnap she-wolves. If they got a hold of her, who knows what the hell they'd do? Especially knowing her connection to me.

I could never live with myself if something happened to her, gods forbid. The fuckers we deal with would take great pleasure in using her to get to me, knowing I'd do anything to protect my mate.

Even now, Blaise's tech guru sits in a cell in the bowels of The Fortress. And I'm bringing her there.

But what choice do I have? None.

The Fortress is the only place for thousands of miles. My ancestors chose this mountain in Greene County north of New York City for its remoteness and built a massive stone structure and surrounding wall straight from Viking times. Only two perilous roads lead to its walls. It's since served as a training and survival facility for our enforcers and a place to interrogate enemies.

We limit The Fortress to the bare necessities—living and technology wise. We're off the grid to maintain a shallow footprint and to lessen the chance of others finding us. A self-contained property with power and plumbing separate from the nearest town. Roughing it to the extreme to ensure our enforcers can thrive in any environment. Tough as nails.

Ordinarily, these conditions serve their purpose. But this freak blizzard took out our power. We're on backup generators with limited areas served. No communication outside of our radios. Not an ideal situation. And damn sure not one for an injured female. But between our resident medic and the she-wolf's healing ability, I expect her condition to improve even while our situation isn't ideal.

As I settle her in front of me on the snowmobile, I glance down at her pinched face. I send a silent prayer to the gods for the trip to The Fortress won't further damage her frail body. As though sensing my thoughts, she whimpers. I wrap an arm around her waist and set off.

I maneuver the snowmobile as efficiently as possible to arrive at The Fortress' imposing ten-feet thick and 40-feet high stone walls.

"Open the gates," I command through my Alpha telepathic bond to the enforcers on gate duty as the snowmobile approaches the first of two portcullises. Immediately, the mighty metal latticed grille lowers, followed by the second one. "Radio Doc to meet me in the infirmary. Now!"

A chorus of "Yes, Alpha" fills my head.

Without hesitation, I plow through the snow and into the inner courtyard. Enforcers rush to my side but stop when I growl low in my throat. A possessiveness I never thought I had outside of my parents, brother, sister, and best friends rises within me. Mine!

The enforcers' eyes widen as their gazes flick between me and the she-wolf in my arms. They back up as I hop off the snowmobile and stride towards The Fortress' double front doors. They cast their eyes down as I pass.

"Doc is heading to the infirmary now, Alpha."

I bite back a growl as a female enforcer opens the

doors. My wolf and I relax a smidgen since she's not a male. I nod in response as I rush inside. She follows me and assists with doors as we make our way through the corridors and down the stairs to the area designated as a hospital.

Despite having the ability to heal on our own, we maintain a hospital in case of unexpected cases that require more than our innate healing can handle. One case being silver as one of the few detrimental things for wolf shifters. But this female needs more help, and I'll be sure she gets all she needs.

Again, the idea of me having a fated mate I can put in danger dampens the pleasure surging through my body. As much as I want to claim this she-wolf as mine, I cannot. The instinct to protect her rides me hard, even if it's against me.

I turn my focus to her, getting better and increase my pace until we arrive at the infirmary.

"What happened, Alpha?"

I tell Doc every detail while a nurse removes my jacket, then cuts the clothes from the she-wolf's body. My cock twitches at the sight of her full tits, narrow waist, and long legs despite the multiple bruises and apparently broken bones. I acknowledge the thought of my now turgid cock tunneling inside of her pussy is not the most appropriate. But I can't help my body's reaction to my mate. Fuck!

Surreptitiously, I adjust my raging erection as Doc begins his exam. He pauses at my feral growl and glances over his shoulder at me. I shake my head and wave my hand to urge him to continue. He cocks an eyebrow.

"Alpha, we can take it from here. You can wait in the outer room," he says.

"No!" I bark, then soften my voice when he jumps. "Get on with your exam. I want to be sure she's fine."

He nods slowly and returns his attention to the she-wolf. I have to bite back more growls as his hands roam over my female's body and she cries out in pain, even with her eyes closed tightly. At first, he hesitates, then ignores my over-the-top possessiveness as his vow to heal others overtakes his Alpha's odd behavior.

What feels like hours but is only a few minutes pass before he faces me.

"She has several broken ribs, an arm, and a fractured ankle. I'm going to give her a CT scan to detect internal bleeding. From the dark blotches beneath the skin of her torso, I fear she may have internal damage. If we need to operate, we will do so immediately. It's surprising her wolf isn't healing her faster. Or perhaps it's keeping her from being worse. We need to move fast, Alpha."

"Do all you must, Doc."

He nods and motions for the nurse. They wheel the gurney from the exam room. I follow, not able to let her leave my sight for one second. He doesn't comment and moves quickly down the corridor to another room.

I stand by the wall, not wanting to get in their way as they shift her to the CT scan table. I watch anxiously as the machine goes through its routine. Each moment my heartbeat increases and sweat forms on my brow. More prayers to the gods to give good news.

At last, the scan completes. Doc reviews the findings, then turns a grim face to me. My heart stutters in my chest. Unconsciously, I press the heel of my palm against the ache in my chest. Gods, please let her be okay. I may not allow myself to complete our mate bond, but I damn sure don't want to lose her. Fuck!

"We need to operate. There's a—"

"Do what you must. Do not let her die."

His mouth opens and closes before he can respond, "Yes, Alpha."

I nod and follow them from the CT scan room to the operating room down the hall. At the double doors, I stop, knowing I can't go in. Instead, I pace. And pray.

DOLPH

"WHAT'S HAPPENING?! Is she all right?!"

Garrett stops mid stride and spins on his heel. Anguish covers his face. My gut roils.

"What the fuck is going on?!"

We pivot to find Colin storming down the hallway. His amber eyes flash gold with his wolf close to the surface. They flick between Garrett and me. An air of aggression surrounds Colin. He stops a foot from us and growls.

"What the fuck are you staring at me like I'm crazy for? Tell. Me. What's. Happening."

His demand causes Garrett to issue a warning growl. It pours from his puffed up chest and bounces off the walls. Electric blue eyes flash with his wolf at the challenging tones from Colin and me. We may be best friends. But something is going on, and we need to figure it out.

"Watch your tones with me."

Colin stops short and narrows his eyes but doesn't utter another word.

I grind my molars to bite back a retort.

Garrett glances through the operating room's window, then turns to us.

"We'll talk in the waiting room," he announces as he strides past us.

Colin grumbles underneath his breath.

I flare my nostrils, trying to get a scent of my fated mate. Immediately, I'm awash with the forest after a spring rain, woody and earthy with a hint of wild honey straight from the comb mixed with coppery blood. Fuck! I growl deep in my chest. My wolf wants to stay by the OR to watch over our mate. But I know I need to hear what Garrett has to say. I take a deep inhalation and pivot on the exhalation.

Neither of my best friends notice my delay in following them to the waiting room. I offer a prayer to the gods and stride on. I push the door open and enter the room.

Garrett crosses his arms over his massive chest with his

feet set in a wide stance. Colin matches him. We stare at one another for a minute before Garrett speaks.

"She's my fated mate."

"The fuck?!"

I shake my head at both of them.

"She's *my* fated mate!"

"How do you figure that?"

Garrett's challenge makes the hairs rise on my neck. My wolf's hackles rise with them. He may be our Alpha. But how dare he question what's mine? And how the hell does he proclaim my she-wolf is his?!

We glare at one another.

"How do you know?"

Colin's murmured question rings loud in the waiting room. My gaze moves to him. His hand rubs his chest right above his heart, as mine has done countless times since I scented the female. Confusion fills his eyes. He flicks them between Garrett and me. Obviously, Colin has no clue what causes the ache in his chest.

I recall as teens how he denied belief in fated mates while Garrett and I confessed our desires to find the she-wolves destined to be ours. Colin laughed and called us wusses who believed in fairy tales. No wonder he has no idea what's happening now. Despite his body telling him by the ache in his chest and undoubtedly the urge in his groin, he does not know.

Jealousy rages through me at the idea they both feel the attraction to my she-wolf as their own. No! She. Is. Mine!

"Not so fast, Dolph!"

I blink at Garrett when I realize I spoke aloud. Dammit!

"She's not yours alone," he says, then continues as he rubs the back of his neck. "What do you smell?"

As I recall her unique scent, Garrett nods knowingly and Colin's mouth drops open in surprise. I search their faces and realize they were born with the same scent embedded in every cell of their bodies as was I.

"No, damn way."

Colin scrubs a hand over his face and groans.

"Please do not tell me she's my—our—fated mate. Is that what this ache in my chest is and the urge to rip anyone apart who even looks at her? To want to protect her at risk of my own life? Is that what you fuckers imply?!"

Garrett looks at me. I look at him. We turn to Colin.

"Yes," we say in unison.

"Holy shit. The gods must be crazy."

Yeah, I'd say…

CHAPTER 6

olin

No damn way.

I stop my pacing to glare at Garrett and Dolph as they wear the floor tiles thin with their combat boots. Both glance at me before shaking their heads and returning to their pacing.

I would never imagine after never believing in fated mates, I find mine in a jet crash. And now she's still in the operating room hours later. No way.

My parents and their parents before them were not destined to be paired. Hell, my mother left my father and me when I was a pup! I know of no one who found their fated mate. But I do understand she's only meant to be with one male.

Now, mine is fated to two males besides me. The only saving grace is we're best friends. And even then, my wolf wants to rip their throats out for even thinking about my female. Damn!

If anyone told me I would have a fated mate and want to kill my best friends on top of it all, I would cut their tongues out and make them swallow it whole. But the gods have their own plans and put Garrett, Dolph, and me in this unheard-of situation. We have the same she-wolf as our fated mate. Whoa.

I run my hands through the longer top strands of my hair for the hundredth time. With a frustrated growl, I resume stomping the floor, my thoughts run rampant.

How the hell will this work out?

Can I share my one true female with my best friends?

What will she think about it?

Hell, will she recover from the crash???

Now that I realize I have a fated mate, I understand my reaction to the injured female and those of the others. We're Alpha male wolf shifters who recognize our female and want her. We just have to figure out how to make this foursome pairing work. And not end one of the other males.

"Listen, I get my wolf wants her. But I can't imagine putting her at risk with the missions we take on. Case in point, the jerk in the dungeons right now. I pray she recovers. But I don't foresee myself claiming her. I won't endanger her. No."

I gawk at Garrett.

"Damn. I hadn't thought about that aspect," Dolph murmurs.

I consider their words. But damn if my wolf doesn't throw his head back and howl in triumph. One down. One to go. But I shake my head. Garrett has a point. And besides, I'm not the most affectionate of the bunch. My dad made sure of that after all the years he complained about my mother leaving him and being bitter about it. He never re-mated.

No wonder I'm all snark—not lovey-dovey, by any means. A cold-hearted bastard, to say the least. One who's caused more pain than others. How could I deserve a happily ever after? While I don't wish harm on the female and hope she recovers, I don't want her either. My wolf howls mournfully.

Sorry, buddy.

"But I can't deny my wolf and I yearn for her. She's our fated mate, and we will claim her in the ancient way of our kind," Dolph adds then rubs his chest. "As long as she makes it out of surgery and heals, gods willing."

"And what if she doesn't want your sorry ass?"

He growls at my retort, and I smirk. Yeah, I'm an unabashed card-carrying alphahole.

"Fuck off, Colin," he snarls as gold glints in his topaz eyes. His wolf ready to burst forth and make me eat my words. I chuckle wickedly.

"Well, I do hope she survives," I say then cock an eyebrow at Dolph as his shoulders sag in relief. "But not so you can mate her. But so she lives. No one's time on this

Earth should end from a plane crash. She's young and deserves a full life."

"I agree," Garrett says with a firm nod then turns to Dolph. "And for the sakes of you and your wolf, I hope she makes it and accepts you, brother. But we still need to find out who she is and what her pack is. She may belong to another, even if they're not fated."

A growl issues from Dolph's mouth as his fists clench at his sides. The temperature in the waiting room rises, baked by his rage.

"Easy, brother, I mean no offense. But as Alpha, it is my duty to put the she-wolf first. I will not allow you to claim her until we have the facts of who she is. But understand, I will have your back either way."

Even my throat clogs at the kind words and Dolph's reaction to them. His eyes soften before he closes them briefly. When they reopen, he nods at Garrett then at me.

"As much as I hate the idea of another male with her, I understand your position. Even if I'd tear the fucker apart if he tries to keep her from me," he says then shrugs when Garrett cocks an eyebrow. "And you may not want a fated mate. But understand I will not deny you claiming her as it's obvious she's meant for the three of us. Don't forget, it's not as though we never shared females before. Despite your reservations, I know as well as you know none of us would ever let any harm come to her. We would protect her with our lives. Three powerful wolf shifters will allow no one to hurt our female. So, don't be so quick to give up on your destinies."

My heart clenches despite my masculine bravado, and I shift on my feet under his piercing stare before he turns it to Garrett, who has a similar reaction. Fortunately, the waiting room door opens, and Doc enters.

DOLPH

"ALPHA?"

The three of us snap to attention even though Doc addresses Garrett. Panic flashes through his wide eyes as his mouth opens, but no sound emerges. He clears his throat and tries again.

"Yes, Doc? How is the she-wolf?"

He tries for a stoic expression with a serious, non-personal tone but fails. His voice cracks at the end.

I glance from him to Colin. His arms fold over his broad chest as his brawny muscles flex beneath his black Henley. He, too, wears a forced expression with an air of indifference.

I know my best friends too well to not recognize the impact our female has on them and on their wolves despite their declarations.

However, I don't have time to analyze them, not when she lies on a metal table in the operating room fighting for her life. I step towards Doc and await his response.

His eyebrows draw together as he sighs. His gaze moves

from one of us to the other before it returns to Garrett, who clenches his fists.

"Well?" He asks, impatience winning over stoicism. "Speak up, Doc!"

He nods and releases another breath.

"She's lucky she's a wolf shifter, otherwise she'd be dead. Impact to the back of her head caused swelling on her brain. She suffered major trauma to her abdomen, specifically ruptures of her small intestine and right kidney and fractured ribs, more than likely because of the seatbelt. A broken ankle and multiple contusions all over her body consistent with jostling during the crash."

"Is she awake?!"

Doc turns to me and shakes his head.

"Her vitals are stable. However, I put her under a medically induced coma to allow her brain and body to heal with the anesthetic, causing a lack of feeling and awareness. Combined with her wolf shifter enhanced healing, I expect improvements in her condition within seven days. She will have round-the-clock monitoring with the nurse and me alternating sessions—"

"I'll help you."

"I'll sit with her too."

Garrett and I speak at the same time. We glance at each other and nod as a silent understanding passes between us. I turn to Colin. He raises his hands palms out and shakes his head vigorously.

"No can do. I have to work on Blaise's techie. You two

can handle one little knocked-out she-wolf without me, right?"

My lip curls with a snarl at his cheekiness. The fucker grins as he salutes and backs towards the waiting room door. He offers a backward wave and leaves.

Garrett clears his throat, and I face him. His eyes remain on Doc.

"Can we see her?"

"Of course, Alpha. But if you don't mind me asking," he pauses then continues when Garrett nods directly his gaze at me. "Did you find anything at the crash site to offer a clue to her identity or that of her pack? It would be good to reach out to them, especially given the extent of her injuries and the chance of recovery. We should make her next of kin aware…"

He trails off as a growl fills the room. His eyes widen, and I realize the sound emanates from me.

I shake my head to get my wolf to back down. Neither of us was pleased to hear any doubt about her recovery. But he's right. Her family must be worried. Too bad we found nothing in the wreckage for the slightest clue.

"Nothing, and the blizzard covered everything up. We'll search again once it dies—"

Garrett cuts his words short at the mention of *dies*. His eyes cut to mine. My heart stutters at the thought of losing our fated mate before we even have a chance to learn her name. I take a controlled breath before I speak.

"I'd like to see her now."

Garrett nods, and we stride towards the door with Doc

behind us. Once in the hallway, he directs us to a patient room with a wall of windows to allow easy viewing of the interior. A nurse sits beside the bed where the still form of the she-wolf lies beneath a blanket. She's so small and helpless, surrounded by medical equipment in a dimly lit room.

Poles with IVs stand at the headboard. The drip tubes lead to her hands placed at her sides. A ventilator mask rests on her face while wires attached to monitors emerge from beneath the white hospital gown. Bruises cover her face and bare arms. Even through the glass, my ears detect the steady beat of her heart and the beeps of the machines.

"Thank the gods she's alive," Garrett murmurs as we near the closed door. He doesn't hesitate to enter. His large frame blocks our female from my view briefly.

I step around him and rush to her side. Instinctively, my hand raises to stroke her cheek. But the bluish-purple marks give me pause. No way do I want to inflict any more pain. My hand lowers to the bed rail and grips it hard enough my knuckles whiten. With my eyes, I scan her body from head to toe.

Rustling across the bed draws my attention. The nurse rises from the chair to allow Garrett room to stand closer to the she-wolf. His eyes never leave our female, even when the door closes behind Doc and the nurse.

Neither of us speaks. Instead, the sounds of our inhalations as we capture her scent join her heartbeat and the beeps. A heaviness weighs down on us as we lose ourselves in our thoughts. Mine focus on the fucked up way we finally meet our fated mate and the despair of losing her before we have a chance to complete our bond. I imagine Garrett's thoughts center on similar concerns. I raise my eyes from her face to his. Our gazes meet across the bed.

"We won't let anything happen to her. We'll be here every step of the way."

I nod in agreement, too choked up to verbalize a response.

~

COLIN

"COME ON, you fucker. You're too much of a wimp to hold out for much longer. Don't think I won't kill you. But first, I'll make you suffer like those she-wolves you and your buddies breed against their will. You'll feel their pain and degradation when your asshole stretches to the point of tearing. You'll sing like a canary."

Blaise's techie whimpers as he squirms naked on a chair. The cane seat ripped out so we have full access to his ass, balls, and cock. Tears stream down his reddened cheeks as one of my enforcers swings the weighted sack under the chair. The techie howls as the sack makes contact with his sac.

I lean in his face and smirk.

"Not so nice, huh?"

He splutters incoherently then gasps when another swing hits him.

"Oh, you'll talk soon. I guarantee."

I rise to my full height of six feet, eight inches and pivot towards the metal table laden with implements to torture the fucker. My fingers trail over a wrench, pliers, saw, pipe, and more. His soft cries increase when I raise a mallet and whack it against my palm.

My thoughts go to the she-wolves we saved and their cries even after we had them safely aboard the helicopters. Their ravaged bodies covered in bruises remind me of the she-wolf in the infirmary. If Blaise and Bernard got their hands on her, they'd breed her against her will.

As much as I don't want to admit she may be my fated mate, my wolf claws under the surface of my skin feral at just the thought of them or anyone harming her. His eyes flash as he bares his long canines. They drip with saliva, hungry to rip the fuckers apart.

For now, we'll settle with this one.

I turn with the mallet and stalk towards him.

"Time to speak up or suffer. You have a choice. The she-wolves didn't."

Focused on his torture clears further thoughts of the female from my mind.

I welcome the distraction since she will never be mine.

CHAPTER 7

arrett

I HAVE MORE PENT up energy than release options. Hand-to-hand sessions with Dolph and Colin are just what I need.

It's been an unbelievable four days. The crazy blizzard still blustering. External communications shot, including our satellite phones. Seriously? An unknown private jet crashes on my mountain. No survivors except for a she-wolf and not just any she-wolf—my fated mate. Or rather, mine, Dolph's and Colin's. What the fuck? Not to mention Blaise's tech guru still holding out despite our convincing tactics. We won't go too hard since we need him alive and talking. How much more will he take? Damn.

And my wolf.

He's driven feral with his need to protect our mate. Always just below the surface, he never rests. Constant pacing, snarling, howling. On edge. I'm running on pure adrenaline and grumpier than ever, as Dolph and Colin tell me.

They're no better.

Dolph doesn't sleep in his rooms anymore. Instead, he placed a cot outside of the she-wolf's infirmary room. If he's not inside holding her hand and talking to her, he stretches out on the cot. And that's only when I'm on bed-watch duty. He knows I nor my wolf want him hovering over the female when it's our turn to care for her.

Colin claimed he wouldn't get involved. But I've caught him in her room, standing in the darkened corner watching her. Only glowing amber eyes reveal his position. So entranced by her, he never hears me enter the room. When he finally sees me, he storms out in silence. Sure he doesn't sense the connection to her.

I do.

But I won't give in, no matter what. As my Alpha duty, I'll keep an eye on her, make certain she has the best care, and once she's awake, find out who she is. If she has a mate or wants to return to her pack, I will ensure she arrives safely. If she senses the mate bond with Dolph, hell, even Colin, and wants to stay with our pack, I'll support them. And pray to the gods to give me enough strength to fight my natural instinct to claim her, too.

Thankfully, we have time before she awakes and decisions have to be made. After this morning's exam, Doc noted her injuries show improvements—slow for a wolf shifter but steady. He assured Dolph and me we shouldn't worry about the pace of her healing. He's confident she's not at the same level of pain and began tapering off the anesthetics for her medically induced coma. After a few days, she'll awake on her own. Then we'll figure out the next steps.

For now, I'll focus my energy on the mat with Dolph and Colin. My mind shifts gears to training as I jog through the warren of underground tunnels beneath The Fortress. Our ancestors built the vast system for routes to escape should enemies breach The Fortress and as a way to enter or to exit undetected.

In recent years, we closed off some tunnels to lessen the maintenance required to upkeep the stone passageways. Most have electricity for lighting, while others still have sconces on the walls for torches. The thick walls block sound. Only the pounding of my sneakers on the stone floor echoes around me. To those unaccustomed to the tunnels, they're hell of eerie.

As pups, we played hide and seek or dared each other to spend the night alone in the darkest tunnels. I can still feel the chill from the dampness and the ghosts of my active imagination. Or were they only in my mind? I chuckle as I approach the doors to the state-of-the-art gym and pull them open.

Immediately, the grunts and growls of male wolf shifters lifting weights, sparring, and doing calisthenics fill the tunnel behind me. The scent of sweat and blood over-powers the cool air of the passageway. Bright fluorescent lights illuminate the stone walls. I step inside, and the doors shut automatically.

A glance around the football field size space reveals areas for free weights and weight training machines, rows of treadmills, rowers, and climbers, heavy and speed bags, and fighting mats and rings. Sections for stretching and mats for exercises round out the space. Doors to the locker rooms with steam rooms, saunas, ice baths, and showers accessed at the furthest corners of the space.

I spot Dolph jumping rope and Colin kicking a heavy bag. As I jog to them, I exchange greetings with the enforcers working out. They appreciate seeing their Alpha sweating right alongside them. The camaraderie keeps our team tight.

"About damn time you showed up. Couldn't pull your-self away from the little she-wolf, Garrett?"

"Fuck off, Colin. Save your shit for the ass whipping I'm about to give you. Let's go."

He smirks and rolls his neck. The bones crack, and his smirk deepens.

"Ready for ya," he grins.

"As am I," Dolph adds with a growl, ever possessive over the female. "And I'll do the ass whipping on both of you fuckers."

"Bring your A game, boys," I snarl as I toe off my sneakers and socks. I toss my t-shirt to the ground and jog onto the center mat. I bounce on the balls of my feet, shaking my head and arms to loosen up. My gaze flicks between the two as they step onto the mat.

The air thickens with tension and male testosterone. The sounds of the others working out diminishes when they notice the hand-to-hand session about to happen. They take places around the mat to watch like spectators at a Mike Tyson boxing match.

Except we don't use a referee. We fight until the other concedes. Only rules, no shifting and no hitting the junk.

"Game. On. Now."

Colin punches his fists together, and the match begins.

Our eyes lock on each opponent as we circle, watching for an opening. Three massive wolf shifters face off. Equal height, weight, and muscle. Except I have the advantage of my Alpha genes in my veins—faster, more agile, quicker thinking.

I see my chance and take it. I rush between the two and with full brutal force, I deliver a roundhouse kick to Colin's left flank and a jab to Dolph's temple.

"Damn... that shit hurts like a motherfucker. Huh?" I taunt as I land on my feet behind them.

"Cocky bastard," Dolph snarls as he comes at me, eyes glowing gold with his wolf.

Before his series of blows can hit me, I quickly crouch low and use my leg to sweep him off his feet. The giant male lands on his ass with an oomph.

"What were you saying, asshole?" I sneer as I do my best Mohammad Ali float like a butterfly sting like a bee moves, cracking my neck side to side.

Then the wind gets knocked out of me.

"Take that. Take that. Take that."

Whap! whap! whap!

An unrelenting succession of blows to my torso reminds me to shut up with the cocky attitude or risk searing body damage. I pivot to the right and land a few punches to Colin's flank. Quick to recover, he roundhouse kicks at my retreating form. I fake left and jab right.

All jokes end as we fight until someone gives. The action of our session is intense. Sweat glistens on our shirtless torsos. Blood splatters on joggers and on shorts. The room rocks with cheers from the enforcers, and our growls and groans. We go at it for an hour before Colin claims victory. He smirks as we stretch and cool down.

"If both of you spent less time worried about that female, you'd focus better and not get your asses handed to you. But even then, I'd still whoop ya," he says.

"Fuck off, Colin," I respond with a growl as I rise.

A frown appears on Dolph's face.

"Shut up and get over your denial already," he sneers and backflips to his feet.

Colin grumbles and jumps up then marches towards the locker room.

"I'm up next for bed-watch duty. So, I'll shower in my rooms," I say and step off the mat without a backwards glance. I don't need Dolph to see the yearning in my eyes for the she-wolf. Colin was right.

Once inside my rooms, I strip out of my t-shirt and joggers. I close my eyes as I duck under the spray from the multiple shower heads and tilt my head back, bracing my hands on the wall. The warm water sluices down my rock-hard body. The ache in my muscles from the strenuous workout lessens. I drop my head and roll my neck, loosening the kinks.

Thoughts drift to the she-wolf—my never-ceasing distraction. I groan as my dick lengthens and the girth thickens. What I would give to bury myself balls deep in her tight, wet heat. I groan again when I think about how it would feel to mount her from behind, lose myself in her pussy, and issue the claiming bite… Damn, instinct drives me hard.

My hand slips from the steam slick wall and slides down the furrow between my eight-pack abs, the well-defined ridges taut under my fingertips. The texture of the trail of hair leading from below my navel to my groin contrasts with my bare skin. I suck in a ragged breath at the vision of my fated mate naked on her knees before me with her eager mouth open wide to receive my ready cock. Her hooded eyes bore into mine, filled with lust.

They're her full lips that wrap around the base of my dick, not my hand, as she takes me down her throat. My forearm-long and wrist-thick cock fills her cavity. Her gag reflex spasms sending a zing to my heavy balls. I squeeze my eyes tight, not wanting to lose the vision before I can blow my load.

Small hands grip my muscular thighs. The fingernails form crescents on my slick skin. Her moans vibrate along my cock and pulsate in my balls. I pull out to the tip, and she pants for air. With a groan, I plunge back in. My bulbous tip hits the back of her throat. Tears fill her eyes as she gags. But she flattens her tongue on the veiny underside of my cock and sucks.

"Such a good girl, taking every inch of my big dick in your little mouth."

Her eyes flutter closed as the corners of her lips lift. The sight of my cock stretching her mouth makes it jump. She hums in carnal pleasure. One hand massages my sac and the other grips and tugs my turgid cock. The rhythm she sets alternates between gentle and painful, keeping a delicate balance that has me close in moments.

I drop my forehead to the slick wall and brace myself on my forearms for what promises to be a leg wobbling experience.

She does not disappoint.

"Fuuuck… Shit, that feels so good," I grunt, as my palms slap the wall.

A pinch to my tip sends me rocking onto the balls of my feet, driving my hips forward to pump against her hand. She senses how close I am to release, so she speeds up her pace.

"Baby," I roar as my dick jumps in her hand and ropes of creamy cum splash onto the wall.

My hips move on their own since she blew my mind right with my cock. She snakes her hand that was on my balls up my torso to pinch my nipple.

Dayummm!

My cock hardens again, and I grab her wrists to pull her

in front of me, facing the wall. I bend her at the waist parallel to the floor and put her hands in place of mine on the tile. I grip my dick and line it up to her slit.

She flicks her long, ebony black hair over her shoulder and lifts her heated gaze to mine. She licks her lips and purrs. Without breaking eye contact, I slam into her tight pussy. Her inner walls greedily suck me in deep. She mewls and lifts to her toes from the force, bowing her back to grant me better access.

I grip her curvy hips tightly and piston into her, chasing our climaxes. I mount the she-wolf, and she bucks against me, meeting each of my thrusts with her own. The sound of our wet skin slapping against each other reverberates in the shower.

I bend my knees and tilt her body back towards mine to change the angle. Her soft, wet curves meld to my hard muscles. As I hit deep within her, she howls her release, her pussy clenching my dick like a vise. I roar and continue my onslaught. She writhes wantonly, demanding more. With unimaginable joy, I give her what she wants.

Our bodies continue the feral dance of the ages until I wrench three more orgasms from her core and she's begging me to stop. Only then do I lower my mouth to the juncture where her neck meets her shoulder.

My extended canines drip with the serum to lodge my scent in her skin permanently—claim her as mine forever. She screams not only from the forceful bite but from the knot on the base of my cock. It inflates behind her pelvis to lock her to me and my seed inside her fertile womb. Her body writhes from the discomfort. I snarl and deepen the bite while I grip her hips until my claws imprint on her skin. I release my load with an almighty feral roar.

Knees give, and I lower to the shower floor turning to settle her on my lap atop my quivering thighs, still intimately connected. Sated at last, I wrap my arms around her, nuzzling her neck and lapping at my mark. Enzymes in my saliva heal the wound. My wolf curls content as he watches our mate.

Then reality hits. I shudder despite the warmth of the steam-filled shower.

"How I wish I could make you mine," I murmur to the emptiness.

igny

"Princess... Princess... wake up..."

"We need you, Baby Girl."

"You're ours, Naughty Girl."

Can I be dreaming? Or do I really hear men's voices? The deep rumble of their baritone rolls over me. It ignites a fire to lick across my skin, straight to my needy core. It pulsates a rhythm that matches my racing heart. The enticing blended scents of sandalwood, vanilla, musk, leather, and spices fill my nose. A moan slips past my lips. Oh, what's happening to me?

More importantly, what are three men doing in my bedroom?

Slowly, I open my eyes and roll over onto my back.

Leaning on my elbows, I stare in the direction of their voices. Even in the darkened room, I can distinguish three sizable frames. But it's their flashing eyes that make my heart skip a beat. I gasp at their unnatural glow—electric blue stands out from the two in gold.

Electric Blue stands at the foot of the bed. A swath of light from the moon crosses his face as the gauzy curtains flutter in the wind. Although I can't decipher enough details to recognize him, I sense his ruggedly handsome face brightens as our eyes meet. Full, kissable lips part as he licks the plump bottom one with the tip of his tongue.

I close my eyes and envision that tongue and mouth on my suddenly engorged clit. A moan slips past the lips on my face even as the lower ones swell with a desperate, aching need.

I've never felt a pull so strong.

An animalistic growl draws my attention to the side of my bed. Gold I bares his unusually long teeth as he frowns at Electric Blue. They glare at one another. Their frames grow larger as muscles thicken. I gasp at their ferociousness. Gold I swings his head to pin me with an intense otherworldly stare.

My pussy clenches. I mewl.

A rumble vibrates in the air and wraps around me. But a snarl from the corner breaks the hold. My wide eyes swivel to Gold II. He stands in the corner. Fists clenched at his sides. The snarl continues past his curled upper lip as his eyes penetrate my soul. He leans forward at my soft cry. But he sways back and shakes his head, holding me captive with his glowing eyes. He chuckles wickedly.

The rumble returns to rouse me from Gold II's hypnotic gaze. Instinctively, my body relaxes as I roll to my back. The comforting sound drowns out the chuckle. I stare up at Gold I.

What's wrong with me that these men excite me? I don't even know them and certainly not enough to have them in my most intimate space. I should be afraid or at the very least demand they leave my bedroom.

He glances down at my bare leg resting atop the sheets, then places one finger on the inside of my ankle. As he trails the tip along my instep, I moan aloud. All thoughts slip away, replaced by carnal desire.

"You've stayed asleep long enough, Baby Girl," he murmurs.

I gasp at the pressure he applies with his knuckle to the sole of my foot.

His eyes flick to my hooded ice blue orbs now darkened with desire. He smirks.

"You captivate us more than you can imagine."

He punctuates each word with a stroke of his knuckle.

The sensation on my erogenous zone morphs from pain to pleasure. My leg jerks as I mewl.

Electric Blue grips my other ankle. Together, they pull me to the foot of the bed, lifting my legs in the air. I end up between their muscular thighs. They flex against my hips.

My ass cheeks hang off the edge. The white silk sheets bunch about my waist. My exposed lower half draws their attention like a magnet. My hips shimmy of their own accord. Feral growls make my pussy clench and flood with my juices. The musky scent of my arousal fills the space between us.

Predatory smiles spread across their faces as their nostrils flare. Their heads tip back as they inhale deeply, eyes squeeze shut. The room plunges into darkness with only the heated glow of Gold II's eyes in the corner. But he advances.

I swallow.

Suddenly, their grips tighten on my ankles in their sizable hands. In one seamless motion, they hoist my hips from the mattress. I hang suspended with my shoulders pressed into the bed. My pussy leaks juices down my thighs to the curve of my ass before they drip to the sheets beneath me. My hands cover my reddened face as I groan. A mixture of carnal lust and embarrassment runs through my heated body.

"Do not hide from us, Naughty Girl."

Firm fingers grip my wrists and pull my hands from my face. I stare up into the gorgeous face of Gold II. His warm breath sweeps over my skin, leaving goose bumps in its wake. He lowers his full lips to my throat. Nips and sucks pebble my nipples even as my pussy gushes more. He chuckles against my sensitive skin.

"You smell so sweet, Naughty Girl."

I mewl as I lengthen my neck to give him better access. He growls appreciatively.

"Don't forget us, Princess."

Hands swat my exposed pussy lips and clit.

Whap. Whap. Whap. Whap.

I howl.

The sting radiates from my core to the tips of my toes and to the top of my head. An electric current of erotic punishment zaps me.

"Do you understand how long we've waited for you?"

"How we ache for you?"

When I hesitate to answer, they spank the sensitive juncture where my thighs meet my ass.

Whap. Whap. Whap. Whap.

My legs flail as I press my hands into the mattress to drag myself away from the punishing tattoo of spanks. To no avail. Trapped by Gold II's arms banded around my shoulders.

"You can dish the pain. But not take it, Naughty. Naughty. Girl? Too bad," he murmurs against the shell of my ear, then chuckles as I shiver.

The pair of burly men set a brutal pace for my punishment. Spanks land on my clit, pussy, sits bones, and thighs. Never landing on the same spot in a row. But not in a distinguishable pattern I can expect. No matter which way I flounder, I can't avoid the blows as Gold II pins me in place. Open-mouthed kisses trail along my collarbones and neck. He brushes his lips over mine. A satisfied groan rumbles in the back of his throat.

My howls increase as each second passes. The time uncountable. The pain unforgettable.

"I—I don't… know what you mean…" I wail.

Tears stream from my eyes to pool in my ears and drip onto the bed below. Chest-racking sobs pour from my slack mouth.

My pussy, ass, and thighs on fire, I submit.

Between howls and sobs, I beg them to answer me.

They continue to spank me.

All tension drains from my body. Still held aloft, I sag. Spent completely. Tears continue to fall but in silence.

More time passes before the spanks change to caresses.

Soft rumblings glide over my skin as all three men soothe me. Their murmurs draw more pleas for answers from me. They lower me onto the bed. Gold II slides me along the bunched sheets until my entire body rests on the mattress, my head on his lap. He strokes my wet cheeks. The other two settle on the bed, bracketing my body. I burrow my face into his thigh as my entire body trembles. Sweat sheens on my skin, and my reddened ass ablaze.

His thick, long dick bulges beneath my cheek. My mouth waters. I turn my head and nuzzle him through his joggers. The cotton soft, his cock hard. It jumps. I moan wantonly.

'You're not forgetting us again, are you?"

My heart skips a beat at Electric Blue's raspy voice.

I raise my head to scan his face.

His eyes glitter in the moonlight like flawless sapphires.

His thumb brushes along my inner thigh. He glides the digit on the wet trail of my pussy juices. My hips buck as I mewl.

"No, never."

A feral grin spreads across his face.

"Good girl."

I bite my lower lip at his praise. But a masculine growl from Gold I draws my attention to him.

He holds my gaze as he lowers his mouth to my other thigh. Instead of his thumb, he uses the flat of his tongue to lave the wet trails all the way to my throbbing core. When he swipes from my puckered hole, past my swollen pussy lips, and up to wrap around my engorged clit, I jackknife from the bed. I keen as an unexpected orgasm races through me.

"So sweet. Like wild honey straight from the comb," he murmurs against my gushing pussy. "I'm going to eat you raw."

He makes good on his promise as he devours my dripping pussy. With each gush, his growls increase in ferocity. Tongue lashes my puffy, slick lower lips sopping up every drop. Teeth nip at the sensitive bundle of nerves. I squeal as more juices spurt into his hungry mouth. My entire body quivers as he groans in male erotic pleasure.

Gold II growls before he slams his mouth over mine, swallowing my passionate cries. The dominating kiss sends tendrils of warmth straight to my heart and soul. Our tongues dance an erotic tango. Flames lick through me. My toes curl as I mold my body to his muscular frame. My hands scrabble along his t-shirt to bring him even closer. The fire between us burns hot.

"Need to be inside you..." Electric Blue growls. Gold II nips at me as he shifts position and grasps my wrists in one sizable hand. He presses them against the mattress above my head.

I lie on my back as the three men hover above me. Mouths drop to my heavy breasts. Tongues lave at the pebbled peaks. I yelp as teeth sink into the sensitive flesh. Tongues flick out to lap the erotic pain away before they suckle each one of my distended nipples.

My head lolls. Cries of passion fall from my parted lips. Pressed flush to my breasts, they hum in pleasure. The vibrations travel through me. I mewl, then my eyes widen as Electric Blue stands to yank his shirt over his head. He tosses it to the floor and grips the placket of his low-slung jeans. The metal buttons pop open to reveal the swollen, purple tip of his massive cock. Commando, his erection springs free.

My mouth waters at the sight of the pearly drop of pre-cum as it glints in the moonlight. I shudder at the realization his turgid girth and length will burn as he thrusts into my little pussy and stretches me to accommodate his big size.

He pushes the jeans past his narrow hips. The muscles in his arms and thighs flex as he wrestles the unwanted material from his body. Standing tall, he fists his cock. The veins stand out in bas-relief. His heavy sac hangs below.

My tongue darts out to lick my lower lip.

He smirks and jerks his cock.

My pussy gushes.

His eyes lower to the apex of my thighs. A carnal smile

tips the corners of his lush mouth at the sight of my glistening pussy lips. The juices slicken my legs. He growls.

In an instant, my hips lift in the air, and my shoulders press into the bed once again. I yelp in surprise. But the Golds hold me firm.

Electric Blue holds me by both ankles. Legs spread wide in a vee. My core aligns with his cock. A snap of his hips, and he impales me on his dick.

I scream from the thick invasion. His tremendous girth fills me. The burn oh so good.

"Fuck!" He roars. Head back, muscles in his neck and arms corded. He stills but for a moment. Then…

"Take. Every. Inch. All of it!"

He pistons balls deep within me, punctuated by each word. My only reprieve when he pulls out to his bulbous tip. His eyes flash as he stares at the blood coating his cock. His nostrils flare. The Golds sniff the air and groan. They bury their faces against my breasts.

Held aloft, I have no choice but to take what he gives to me as he continues to plow into my pussy. And I take it with absolute pleasure.

I writhe beneath him screeching like the cat in heat I am.

Fuck, he feels so damn good…

The slapping of skin on skin with the squelch of my pussy juices mixes with his grunts and groans and my cries. The erotic chorus arouses me like no other symphony. They spur him on to fuck me into the bed. It groans in protest.

"Oh! Oh! Yeeessss!" I shout as a powerful orgasm rips through me.

A flash of white light sparks behind my eyelids, squeezed shut as ecstasy rolls over me. My inner walls tighten around his pulsating cock. He growls and pummels harder. Unstoppable. Relentless.

The Golds join in his feral beast-like groans while mine mix in for an erotic composition.

Booms blast and bright lights explode with each of the countless orgasms he forces from my ravaged core.

Sweat drips from his forehead to trail between my bouncing breasts as he leans over my torso. The Golds move aside, stroking my arms. His dominant hands wrap under me to grasp my thighs as he changes the angle of his savage thrusts. His firm pecs drag over my taut nipples. Guttural groans and growls fill my ear as he chases his release.

As his cock swells impossibly larger, his body judders. Hot breath puffs across my sweat-drenched neck into my damp hair.

"Mine!"

His carnal cry and the copious amounts of his cum bathing my pussy trigger another epic climax.

I scream in pleasure as my eyes roll back and my back bows.

He collapses on top of me. I bear his heavy weight happily. The last vestiges of his release drip from my core, down my ass cheeks to the drenched sheets below.

I scream as pain laces around my throat. He growls as

his teeth bury deeper into my flesh. The Golds hold my arms out to the side, preventing me from breaking free. They growl and snarl like wild animals. Hot saliva drips from inhumanly long teeth onto my bare arms. I cry out in alarm even as my pussy clamps around his cock, milking him of his seed.

"Mine!"

"Mine!"

The Golds chorus in savage voices with nostrils flared before they lower their mouths to my neck as Electric Blue lifts his face and stares down at me. His cock still buried deep in my pussy.

"You are now ours, Princess."

My mouth opens in a silent scream.

Darkness descends.

CHAPTER 9

"So sweet. Like wild honey straight from the comb," he *murmurs against my gushing pussy. "I'm going to eat you raw."*

"Oh! Oh! Yeeessss!"

"Mine!"

"You are now ours, Princess."

What the hell?!

I jolt awake, growling barbarically with my canines extended dripping serum and my engorged cock hard as steel leaking pre-cum. My heated body thrums. Rapid pulse pounds in my ears. Eyes flash gold as my wolf fights to break free, to take control, to mate.

Wrestling to maintain dominance, I gnash my teeth with a snarl. The giant golden wolf narrows his flashing eyes and paws the ground. We face off, neither willing to back down. I draw on my innate Alpha and force my wolf to retreat. Only one of us will ever be in control. And that's me.

I swing my legs off the cot and glance over my shoulder through the windows to the she-wolf's infirmary room. She lies still. No sign of the sexy siren in my dream. And what a dream.

My hand grips the back of my neck as I crack it from side to side. Sexual tension still rides me even as the dream dissipates. My cock long and thick pulsates on my thigh, eager for me to bury it in the she-wolf's sweet pussy. Hell, it may have been a dream. But I damn sure taste her on my tongue. It slides over my lower lip as though savoring the remnants of her pussy juices. Delectable.

I close my eyes, trying to hold on to the last vestiges of the dream. Nostrils flare to catch a final whiff. My mouth waters as her unique scent glides along my tastebuds. A throaty groan escapes as I exhale.

But my dick is still hard.

A glance over my shoulder confirms the she-wolf sleeps. Another down the hall reveals no one present. Good. I untie the string on the waistband and slide the low-slung joggers down my thighs. Once again, I groan. This time in relief as my aching cock springs free and my heavy balls hang loose.

Without hesitation, I fist the thick base and squeeze. My head lolls back as my eyes close. Instantly, images of the she-wolf writhing on the bed as I ate her sweet pussy appear. My cock jumps in my hand. More pre-cum leaks from the tip. It drips down the shaft. I use the natural lubricant to coat the head and slide my fist to the base.

Her low and guttural moans fill my ears. Her tantalizing scent suffuses my nostrils.

On a growl, I vigorously pump my cock and thrust my hips up with my muscular thighs spread wide, heavy balls bounce between them. I don't stop until ropes of my creamy cum jettison like a geyser in a series of powerful spasms. I throw my head back as I squeeze my eyes shut and roar. The vision of my girth stretching her pussy as my canines pierce her neck for my claiming bite appears in my mind.

The intensity of my release ricochets through my body. My heated skin tingles. Spots appear behind my closed eyelids. The weight of my head proves too much as the lightheaded sensation takes over. My curled toes relax as I allow myself to recover.

A possessive grin spreads across my face. My Baby Girl may be in a coma. But her mind and body sense her fated mates near.by And I cannot wait to make her mine.

COLIN

"MINE!"

Blood fills my mouth.

I sputter as the tangy fluid pours down my throat. I roll to my side, coughing. My lower lip throbs from deep puncture wounds. The coopery scent of fresh blood fills my nostrils as I struggle to catch my breath.

My head swivels to take in my surroundings. The familiar shapes of my furniture let me know I'm in my set of rooms at The Fortress, not in a bedroom. Only me amidst the strewn sheets. The bed empty of the she-wolf and damn sure of Garrett and Dolph.

What the hell just happened? Why did it seem so real I bit my lip thinking the female's throat was in my mouth? And why the hell is claiming serum mixed with the blood???

My mind plays back to the dream. The three of us primed to claim the she-wolf, permanently mark her with our scents beneath her skin so all males know she is ours. The bite marks visual proof for them to stay away from her even before they catch our scent.

But that's far from what I want.

Isn't it?

Not according to my howling wolf. His massive tawny head thrown back as he calls to his mate. I sense his need to complete the mating bond as surely as I feel it in my throbbing dick.

It's harder than a diamond.

I glance down at it.

The platinum beads of the deep shaft reverse Prince Albert piercing gleam. The plum-shaped tip an angry red and shiny with pre-cum pokes from the waistband of my shorts. My cock lays heavy along my eight-pack abs to above my navel.

Might as well give myself some relief.

I spit in my hand and palm the head to slicken my cock as I fist it and glide to its base. My husky growl fills the air. So amped from the dream, it won't be long for me to blow my load.

My head drops back against the pillows of the big empty bed. I let my imagination run wild with ways to fuck the she-wolf. I envision her on all fours—ass high and head low. Her pretty pink pussy glistens as her puckered hole winks. She shimmies her hips to taunt me and my beast. It works.

We pounce on her. She yelps as our claws grip her ass cheeks and spread them. Wide. Held in place, she can only take what we give her, and it'll be a mounting she'll never forget. Our dripping cock strokes her from her swollen clit to her soaking pussy, gathering the juices from her puffy lips before demanding entrance to her puckered hole. She hisses as the tip breaches the first tight ring of muscle. But we don't stop.

"Relax and take every inch, Naughty Girl."

She whimpers even as she pushes back against me, impaling herself on my cock. We groan in unison as her tight inner walls clamp my cock like a vise from root to tip.

"Fuuuck…"

Inch by agonizingly slow inch, I withdraw from her heat until only the tip remains embedded. She mewls and tosses her ebony hair. The glossy strands slide along her waist and cover her shoulders. I gather her hair into one fist and tug as I snap my hips forward. She screams as my big cock burrows inside her little hole. Pants follow then lusty moans as I roll my hips against her round ass. I press my front against her back, caging her in with my hands on either side of her head. I circle my hips.

"You take my cock so well, Naughty Girl."

She moans long and low as I murmur in her sweat-dampened hair.

Then I drill her into the mattress. Her carnal cries mingle with my feral groans. Skin slaps against skin. The musky scent of animalistic fucking surrounds us, filling our nostrils. She matches me thrust for thrust, urging me on.

My fist works my cock. I grunt as my balls draw up.

Damn, I want my dick buried deep within her tight ass, lost in bliss as her inner walls milk every drop from it. Damn!

Hot streams of cum shoot all over my bare chest, pecs, and abs tight with tension. Eyes squeeze shut. My body shudders from the power of my orgasm. Now, I pant and moan.

Oh, little she-wolf, what have you awakened in me?

~

Garrett

· · ·

"You are now ours, Princess."

I jerk upright. Sweat drenches my taut body. It drips in rivulets down my pecs and along the ridges of my eight-pack abs. Its salty musky scent blends with the forest after a spring rain, woody and earthy with a hint of wild honey straight from the comb. Her unique scent. The she-wolf who invades my dream.

A fated mates dream.

They say fated mates can have dreams about the other. The more frequent and intense they become, the closer the pair gets to their first encounter. A sort of bonding before the actual mate bonding ceremony occurs. In the dreams' vividness, the pair appear to be together in reality, not a dream—wet or otherwise. Sometimes they recognize one another. Often, they're not revealed, somehow shrouded or in wolf form.

This one?

I clearly saw the female. And Dolph and Colin. No mistaking who was present—or why. We wanted to claim her. So, we did. The crazy thing is she accepted it. Three males as her mates, not one. She showed no fear or hesitancy. Her arousal still lingers in my nose. Her cries of ecstasy music to my ears. And my cock.

It throbs to the sensuous rhythm as though still buried balls deep inside of her tight, wet pussy. Can she be a virgin? My dick jumps, bobbing yes.

I scrub a hand over my face.

Cut it, Garret, and focus.

A few deep, cleansing breaths clear my mind of the

lascivious thoughts of fucking and claiming a comatose female. But it's not like I came up with it. The gods do strange things, including dreams between destined pairs. A precursor of what's coming—no pun.

So, maybe she is a virgin. My wolf's tongue lolls from his mouth as his eyes flash electric blue.

"Enough!" I growl and jump from the bed.

If I lived the dream, she must have too. Instead of lusting after her, I need to check she's all right. Hell, she may even be awake. The power of the dream sure as hell woke my ass up.

As I stalk from the bedroom, I will my eager dick to calm down. It bounces heavily along the length of my thigh beneath my joggers. Fortunately, they're heather gray and camouflage the pre-cum as it drips from my tip. I can't help the thick outline of the shaft and the mushroom-shaped head.

By the time I reach the infirmary, my cock is the least of my worries. Dolph and Colin stand nose to nose. Testosterone scents the tension-filled air. They smell of cum and sweat. Just like me. As I suspect, they experienced the mating dream, too. Still hyped by claiming the she-wolf, they don't move even as I approach.

"Okay, what the hell is going on?"

"Tell this fucker to back the hell up. I have as much right as he has to enter the she-wolf's room," Colin snarls as his fists clench at his sides.

Yeah, the gods are crazy, making three Alpha wolf

shifters share a mate. I scowl. Two. Not me. I shake my head and focus on the two butting chests.

"Fuck off, Colin. You said you want nothing to do with her," Dolph snaps.

I push them apart and glare from one to the other.

"Get a damn grip. Now!"

I put Alpha command behind my words.

They lower their gazes to the floor.

"You experienced the mating dream, as did I. We were harmonious in the dream. Real life? Not so much, obviously," I say as my gaze moves between them. They raise their eyes, and I continue. "Listen, I don't know whether or not the dream will come true, especially since we do not know who she is and her status—"

"Doesn't matter. She's not the one."

I cock an eyebrow at Dolph.

"Her choice. Period."

"Whatever. I just want to see if she's okay. Thought she may have woken up," Colin says, then strides to the door.

We follow him inside.

Then freeze.

Each of us growls as the powerful scent of her sweet, musky arousal smacks us in the faces.

The hairs on my jet black wolf ripple as he leaps to his giant paws and charges forward. Eyes flash electric blue as his jaws gape. Serum drips from the canines. His growl emanates from my mouth.

Dolph and Colin react similarly as we stare at our fated mate.

The she-wolf lies in bed. No movement. But her flushed cheeks intrigue me. With the anesthesia at a lower dose, her mind must be coming back online. She must have felt something.

Colin coughs to clear his throat.

"Looks fine to me," he says in the raspy voice of his wolf. He coughs again and continues. "Go back to guard-dog duty, Dolph."

The sexual tension in the room decreases even as he growls at the snarky remark. But the alphahole of the bunch chuckles as he leaves the room with a backward wave.

I rein in my savage beast, then turn my attention back to the she-wolf. I scan the machines. Certain there's no other changes, I cast a last glance at her. I clap Dolph on the shoulder and stride from the room. A glance over my shoulder shows him unmoving at the foot of the bed, staring at her.

Gods help us.

Or we're all fucked.

CHAPTER 10

 *olin*

I DON'T KNOW what draws me to the she-wolf's room.

But I'm glad I took a break from Blaise's loyal dog—the SOB hasn't broken in over a week—since Dolph ditched his guard-dog duty. The comatose she-wolf is all alone. Not cool. At. All. I have words for him and Doc when I leave here.

I enter her room.

A sense of peace washes over me as I inhale her unique scent. As much as I don't want a mate—fated or otherwise —I can't deny my attraction to her. The dream from the other night and more since convince me she's my destiny. But I won't give in. Nor will I admit it to Garrett and to Dolph. No.

Her prone form continues to rest on the bed, undisturbed and supported by machines. Doc assures us her healing progresses, even if it's slower than normal for wolf shifters. But if her appearances in these *fated mate dreams*—as Garrett and Dolph call them—prove anything, then she's in top shape.

My cock jumps, and my wolf growls in agreement. Both have thoroughly enjoyed the lifelike nightly visions. Waking with a raging hard-on or smothered in sticky cum should ease the constant ache in my chest. But they don't.

Sadly, this godsforsaken blizzard continues to drop snow nonstop. I can't even release the pent-up sexual frustration with a run through the forest in wolf form. We're all stuck inside The Fortress. The only saving grace being bouts in the gym. Oh, and sessions with Blaise's boy wonder. However, today's session did little to ease the tension.

But a whiff of the she-wolf's scent eases it. I roll my shoulders and stretch my neck, shaking off any thoughts unrelated to her wellbeing. My eyes scan the machines and IVs to ensure they function properly. Beeps sound steady. Medication and nutrients drip. Her chest rises and falls with the ventilator. Nothing amiss.

My eyes lift to her face. The bluish-purple bruises faded to yellow with less swelling. More sun-kissed skin than pale shows through. Her lower lip is still swollen. But more from the natural fullness of her lush mouth than the busted lip. Despite the nutrients, she's lost weight. Shadows form along her pronounced cheekbones. Yet, no one can deny her beauty.

My fingers itch to stroke her heart-shaped face. Drag the pad of my thumb over her plump lips. Push the tip into her mouth. Would she suck it?

You know what, Colin, stop fantasizing over a comatose female, you freak!

I scrub a hand over my face and stalk to the farthest corner. I'll watch over her from there, far enough away I can't touch her. Somebody has got to take care of her. I guess I'm on guard-dog duty today.

SIGNY

WAKE UP.

An alert goes off in my mind.

I'm not alone.

My body doesn't want to cooperate as I try to lift my head from a pillow. It's heavy as lead, too much for my neck to lift. My eyes flutter open to a darkened room. Machines beep. Panic grips me in the unfamiliar space. It's too much.

"Who's there?"

My mind thinks I spoke clearly. But my ears pick up, *Whawhawhawha.*

I whimper in frustration.

A whoosh of air brings the aroma of leather, spices, and musk. It engulfs me. My breath catches in the back of my throat. I gasp.

Golden eyes glow at the foot of the bed.

"What's wrong?"

The smokey timbre rolls over me. Goose bumps erupt over my suddenly hot and tight skin.

Where do I recognize his voice from? Why does his aroma evoke desire in me?

Questions bounce around my head as my body reacts of its own accord. It's too much all at once.

My eyes close as his move closer.

"What the hell did you do to her?!"

Another familiar aroma sweeps into my nose. This one wraps me in a warm velvet blanket. My busy mind relaxes as it drifts away.

SIGNY

"—CHANGE in her eyelids fluttering mean? Is she dreaming?"

"Why has her breathing changed? I can detect an increase in her heartbeat."

"The other night, her cheeks turned red."

My mind trudges through molasses as I try to make sense of what I'm hearing. A heaviness weighs on my torso.

None of my limbs move despite my brain's demands. White light shines behind my closed eyelids. Too bright.

What the hell is wrong with me?!?!?!

The voice fades in and out as I try to make sense of this world I'm trapped in.

Pain shoots through my heavy head; a dull pounding beats in my ears; blackness alternates with a spark of light beyond my sealed eyes.

"Female, can you hear—"

"Yes!" I scream, but the word rattles in the back of my throat. *Whawhawhawha.* My thick, dry tongue sticks to the roof of my mouth. I try to cough, swallow, but nothing happens.

"Can you hear me?"

That voice. I've heard it before. My mind plays back but only fragments, bits, and pieces of—

I gasp as images of me in dozens of sexual positions flicker movie-like. Held aloft as two men pummel my pussy and ass while I fist another man's giant cock. Mounted by one man with another's cock in my mouth and another beneath me suckling my breasts. My pussy spasms and nipples bead. What the absolute hell???

What's going on? In fact, where the hell am I?

Growls cut through the molasses, pushing the viscous goo to the edges of my mind as I try to make sense of my surroundings. If only briefly.

Another flash of pain wipes any response, no matter how feeble. Acid burns as it rises from my belly. Bile fills my mouth. I choke.

Help. Me.

Arms lift me from the pillow. Hands dab tissues on my face. Snarls surround me.

"—Alpha, please. Beta, Colin. Let me get closer to exam her—"

"Careful now, Doc."

"She's in distress!"

"What did you do to her?!"

"Alpha, allow me."

A woman's voice cuts through the men's argument.

Gentle hands grasp cradle my head and support my back as I'm lowered to the pillow on my side. A bit of bile seeps from my mouth. Tissue dabs my chin.

"Easy, now. You're waking up. Breathe slowly through your nose."

Her calm demeanor contrasts to the anxious tones. My heartbeat slows as I do as she suggests. She rubs my arm as she speaks comforting words. But I need answers.

With an effort, I part my lips.

"W—W—Where... am I?"

This time a coherent question, and it's enough to get someone's attention.

"You're in the infirmary, and I'm a doctor. Allow me to exam you first, and we will answer your questions..."

The unfamiliar voice says more, but I tune him out after *doctor. Infirmary?* What happened to me?

I don't have time to contemplate the situation as the doctor begins the exam and the female—who I assume is a nurse—helps. I notice soft casts on an arm and an ankle.

Aside from my head, my ribs ache. What the hell happened?

"Excellent. I'm going to use my penlight to check your responsiveness. Don't attempt to speak yet," the doctor says.

When he lifts my eyelid, pain slices through my skull from a blinding light. I groan and turn away.

Immediately, the three men berate and threaten the doctor. He tells them he didn't mean to hurt me and explains why the light bothered my eyes. They grumble for him to be careful or else.

Who are they?

The room dims.

"My apologies. Your eyes are sensitive to light at the moment. Keep your head still for now. We'll give you medication to ease the discomfort," the doctor says as I pick up movement from my left. The three men murmur amongst themselves.

The exam continues with minimal interruption from them until the doctor announces I need privacy so he can check my body without the gown.

"We need to watch what you're doing, Doc."

"No."

"Privacy? We've already seen her naked."

"What?" I gasp. My eyes fly open. I stutter.

The three men from the erotic dreams stand at the foot of my bed. Their eyes flash electric blue and gold. It's uncanny how they materialized from the ethos to the real world. Or am I still dreaming? My body shudders.

I thought their voices sounded familiar. I just couldn't place them with things being so hazy. What. The Hell. I thought I had questions before. Now, a million run through my mind.

"Who are you, and why can't I remember anything but you in my dreams???"

My voice rises to a frantic pitch as my eyes flick from one man to the next. I thought it was a figment of my imagination, a carryover from my erotic dreams. But no. Their eyes glow—Electric Blue, Gold I, Gold II—as they stare back at me.

Trapped by their intense eyes, I can't look away. And damned if my nipples don't pucker as my chest heaves with the increase of my breath from the racing of my heart. The rapid pulse beats an erotic staccato in my heated blood as it blazes through my aroused body.

The air in the room skyrockets as the men growl deep in their broad chests that appear to increase in size with each passing second. Their tongues dip out to lick their full lips—soft and moist like my lower lips. Their nostrils flare as their growls pitch lower. I swear the vibrations reach my pussy and swirl around the pulsating walls, licking every inch.

I shudder.

"Excuse me."

The doctor's voice cuts through the lust fog.

The four of us blink as one. We shift our gazes to him.

His eyes flick from one to the other. At Gold I's growl,

the doctor swallows audibly. He lowers his gaze to the floor.

"What?" Electric Blue demands.

The doctor lifts his eyes to respond.

"Alpha, allow me to ask about her memory. She says she can't remember anything but... Ah... you in her... Uh... dreams."

His gaze drops as he stutters over the dreams.

Hell, I don't blame him. If only he knew what they entailed, he'd do more than stumble over mentioning them. They'd render him speechless!

"Wait, what?" Gold II's head snaps to me. "Do you know your name? Where you come from? Your pack?"

My eyebrows pinch together.

With the distraction of sexual tension gone, I search my mind for answers. Nothing but the erotic dreams appears. I probe deeper as fear grips my chest. Name... Name... Name. Blank.

Why can't I remember? What happened to me? Where am I? Who am I???

"Breathe. Just breathe. Follow along with me."

A strangled sob falls from my mouth.

I didn't realize I spoke aloud.

My eyes pop open to find the nurse before me. Soft brown eyes meet my frantic ice blues. She clasps my hands and repeats her words before she exaggerates her breaths. I nod as I take a deep breath then sync with her.

While we breathe, urgent whispers begin. My gaze

shifts, but she squeezes my hands to center me again. Once my heart doesn't bang in my chest, she smiles.

"You did well. Remember to just breathe whenever something overwhelms you. Okay?"

"O—Okay. Thank you."

She steps away as Electric Blue moves around the side of the bed closer to me.

He exudes immense power and raw masculinity. Silky jet black hair, chiseled cheekbones, firm jaw. Glacial blue eyes lock on me. Apparently, they change color when his emotions run high, like in my erotic dreams where he stars.

Stop it! I chastise myself mentally. I squeeze my eyes shut with a frustrated sigh. It's imperative I ignore the flutters in my lower belly at his nearness. Answers rank higher than lust.

When I open my eyes, his full lips quirk as though he reads my mind. A mind that holds no answers for me. He crosses his muscular arms over his well-defined pecs and cocks his head.

"I am Garrett Moen, Alpha of the New York Wolves Pack. You are safe in The Fortress within our territory. A week ago, the private jet you were on crashed not far from—"

I gasp and shake my head. Once again, the room closes in on me, and my heart bangs against my ribcage as I pant and squeeze my eyes shut. *No! No! No!*

Warm, sizable hands grasp my wrists and pull my hands from my face. The calloused thumbs rub my knuckles.

"Breathe, Baby Girl, breathe with me."

I don't have to open my eyes to recognize the comforting voice and musky aroma of Gold I. A calm settles over me as I mimic his steady breaths.

"Good girl," he murmurs when I open my eyes. "I'm Dolph Pihl."

Dolph. It's a though a golden halo surrounds him with his buzzed blonde hair and gleaming topaz eyes. His clean-shaven cheeks and jaw highlight the masculine bone-structure of his gorgeous face. Even more so when his full lips curve into a breathtaking smile.

Another gasp. But this one leans towards the carnal side.

I shake my head. Not now. Focus.

"A crash? Was I alone?"

Dolph glances at Garrett. They seem to share an internal communication. Then Garrett speaks.

"No, four others were with you. From what we could determine, three male wolves and a she-wolf. We gave them proper burials—"

"Oh, no…"

Tears blur my vision. They spill down my cheeks as I shake my head over and over again. A growl from the foot of the bed halts my movements. I blink as Dolph swipes the tears with his fingers. But it's Gold II who captures my attention.

His eyes flash between amber and gold. His stubbled jaw clenches. I'm drawn to his ferocious beauty—sharp angles of his nose, cheeks, and jaw softened by long tawny eyelashes and full lips. Like the other two men, he's at least a foot taller than my five feet, eight inches, with an Adonis body.

"Stop. Hurting. Her."

He bites out the words as he flicks his gaze over the others.

"It's all right, Colin. She'll have to know the truth. Better to get past it."

Colin narrows his eyes at Garrett but says no more. Garrett turns to me.

"We couldn't find any identification for any of you. Are you sure you don't remember your name or your pack?"

Pack? Wolves? She-wolf?

"Why do you keep mentioning wolves and packs? What do you mean?"

He frowns and glances at the doctor. Again, it seems as though they communicate silently as their facial expressions alter during the exchange. The doctor turns to me.

"You suffered trauma to your head which explains your memory loss. It more than likely is temporary. The medically induced coma lasted for seven days. But your mind requires more time to heal completely. I will run more tests now. Then you will rest."

He nods at the nurse, and she steps forward. Garrett, Dolph, and Colin move to the opposite wall as the doctor and nurse release the brakes on the bed. As they roll me towards the door, I raise my hands.

"Wait! Answer me!"

The bed rolls to a stop. Ignoring the pain, I shift to face

the three men. The whole erotic dreams featuring them, wolves, packs. My mind may have lost memories. But it damn sure knows when something feels off. And the prickles along the back of my neck confirm it.

I focus on Garrett since he's their leader. He returns my stare.

"All of us are wolf shifters. We have human and wolf forms with the ability to shift between the two at will. The human form dominates the inner wolf and remains in control, even in wolf form. We live in packs with territories under our specific control, led by Alphas."

Tears pool in my eyes.

My head tilts back as my body quakes.

Uproarious laughter bubbles up as the tears slide down my heated cheeks.

I fan a hand over my face as I return my gaze to Garrett.

"Get… outta… here…"

He shakes his head and sighs.

Dolph raises an eyebrow.

Colin grips the back of his t-shirt and yanks it over his head. He drops it to the floor as his fingers rip open the placket of his black cargo pants. He shimmies them down his muscular thighs then stands. In. All. His. Naked. Glory.

My mouth drops open as saliva gathers on my tongue. My eyes widen as my lust-filled gaze travels the length of his sculpted body. Bronzed skin changes to deep pink at his ginormous erect penis. The erotic dreams did not lie. At. All.

The crackling of bones reshaping and muscles lengthening fill the room. A flash. An immense tawny wolf appears on all four giant paws within moments. His massive head swivels towards me as his eyes spark golden. The beast prowls forward.

I gasp as darkness descends.

igny

"—DID you up and shift like that?"

"You made her faint from fright! Pretty fucked up, even for you, Colin."

"Oh, bite me. Both of you! Didn't you say she needed to know the truth? Well? You can't get any closer to the truth than for her to see our wolves."

Whisper-shouting awakens me.

It takes a moment to reorient myself as my eyes open. I flick my gaze left and right until it finds Garrett, Dolph, and Colin. The doctor and nurse aren't in the room any longer. A part of me wishes they were, especially the nurse since my pulse races again. I close my eyes and breathe through my nose slowly.

In. Out. In. Out. In. Out.

My eyes open on the exhale.

The trio stare at me from the foot of my bed. Again.

Fortunately, Colin stands as a man and not a bigger-than-a-car wolf. My body trembles as I recall his predatory stare. Would he eat me alive? My pussy, yes.

A hysterical laugh bursts from my mouth. I clap my hand over it as the trio frown.

"I apologize for Colin's thoughtless behavior."

"Are you all right?"

Garrett and Dolph speak at the same time. Colin shrugs. I narrow my eyes at the alphahole, and he winks. A growl slips past my curled lip.

Once again, I slap my hand over my mouth, stunned by the animalistic sound coming from me. Me! What the hell?!

Colin chuckles wickedly.

"On the surface, you may not remember. But your wolf remains in there somewhere," he snarks. He licks his lower lip and continues. "You can thank me later, *Princess*."

The term doesn't remind me of the endearment expressed by Garrett in my erotic dreams. Instead, it's sarcastic. My eyes narrow again. Colin reacts with another chuckle.

"Stop teasing her, Colin," Dolph growls. Then he turns to me and smiles. Instantly, I relax. "Don't worry. Doc tells us it's not unusual for someone to suffer memory loss after a severe head injury. You have time to recover fully. There's nowhere to go with the blizzard still raging. We're buried pretty deep now. And we can't communicate with any other packs since the storm knocked out the signal. You're safe here with us."

"Safe? With you wolves running around? I don't think so," I retort. My knees draw up to my chest, and I wrap my unbroken arm around them. My chin rests on top as I stare at the trio.

What type of situation am I in? If Colin hadn't morphed into a wolf, I would think they were lunatics or joking with me. This just isn't plausible.

No memory and trapped in a building during a blizzard with wild beasts on the loose? Even if they are sexy as sin, they're still scary as all hell. How can it get any worse?

Then I chide myself. The other four in the plane didn't survive. I'm sure they'd rather be in my position, even if it's fantastical. And dangerous.

"W—Will you eat me?"

The question slips out before I can pull it back. My cheeks heat, and I lower my gaze.

Naturally, Colin chuckles.

I ignore him, even if my pussy throbs.

"Not in the way you think. You experienced the dreams," Garrett smirks.

I lift my gaze to him, and he waits for me to nod before he continues.

"For our kind—and you are a wolf shifter too—the dreams are experienced between fated mates or those destined by the gods to bond for eternity. The dreams represent what's coming, foretelling the pair's connection—"

"One, I'm not a 'wolf shifter,' some freak of nature. Two, a pair, not a reverse harem!"

He only nods at my outburst.

Dolph flinches.

Colin glares.

"I don't want anything to do with you, anyway. So, I'll take my 'freak of nature' ass to the dungeons. I have more important shit to do than to listen to a whining, no-memory-having she-wolf," he snarls and strides from the room.

I flinch. Pain lances through my heart. I rub my chest as I watch him leave. Why is he such an alphahole? I shake my head and turn to the other two.

Dolph glances at Garrett.

"And what's with the silent communication? That's what you're doing, isn't it?" I grumble irritably.

"Yes. As Alpha of the pack, I can communicate with pack members telepathically over short distances. I share a bond with each one, similar to the bond between mates."

I sigh and shake my head. Too weird. But a man just changed into a wolf, so…

"We understand your frustration and disbelief. Expected given your memory loss. However, you can't deny we shared mating dreams. Thus, your connection to us. As. Your. Fated. Mates. Yes, more than a pair is unusual. But it's not unheard of, just rare. As you have time to heal, we have time to get to know one another. In the flesh. Okay?"

I study Dolph's face.

He's so sincere. His eyes shine with hope. A hesitant smile curves the corners of his mouth.

I want to believe him. But…

"How do you know I'm a wolf shifter? Your fated mate? Aside from the dreams. You've shown me proof you—or at least Colin—can transform into a wolf. I need proof about… us."

Dolph opens his mouth to answer.

But Garrett's deep baritone vibrates through the air. It ripples over my skin while his heated eyes caress my face and body. Electric blue eyes back on mine. He inhales, nostrils flare, eyes flash.

"Your unique scent. The forest after a spring rain, woody and earthy, with a hint of wild honey straight from the comb. It's imprinted on our brains, marking you as the one—for each of us," he responds, ending in a growl.

The vibrations reach a peak, and my pussy gushes.

My cheeks redden when they tip their heads back and sniff audibly. Deep drags draw into their lungs. If they're wolves, they must have a keen sense of smell. My face flames, realizing they must detect my arousal. Grins that can only be described as feral spread across their faces. I duck my face behind my knees.

"And our wolves recognize the one hidden within your soul. She is their mate, too."

Dolph's words come out thick with raw need. I mewl when his fingertips skitter over my bare arm, then pant when he lifts my hand to his mouth and licks the sensitive underside of my wrist. A jolt of lightning skates up my arm straight to my heart. I inhale sharply as my eyes widen in surprise.

"They can taste your wolf on your skin," he growls, as his eyes spark golden.

I startle and gasp at the sudden knock on the door.

Both men growl as their heads swivel to the door.

It opens to the doctor and nurse. They pause as their eyes flick from one man to the other before focusing on me. The doctor nods decisively before he faces Garrett.

"Alpha, I hate to disturb you. But it's imperative we run the tests. Now."

Garrett's eyes narrow. He glances at me. I stare back and blink. He turns to the doctor and nods.

"Fine. I have business to attend to. Inform me of the results immediately," he grumbles then turns to me. "Press one on the phone beside your bed for a direct line to me. Call should you need anything. Understand?"

I nod.

He cocks an eyebrow.

Something inside of me says to address him properly. A wisp of a breath slips past my lips.

"Yes, Alpha."

His glacial blue eyes darken to cobalt as his nostrils flare on a sharp inhalation. A second later, he schools his face and pivots on his heel.

Once again, a pang to my heart has me rubbing my chest as the second of the three men leave my room. An unexpected sense of loss sweeps over me.

A squeeze of my hand brings my attention to Dolph. He smiles at me gently.

"I'll be on my cot right outside of your room when you finish the tests. I won't leave you, Baby Girl," he says, ending with a rumble.

It reaches deep inside of me to soothe my soul. Tears fill my eyes.

So much has happened, and I do not know who or what I am and we're I'm from. But somehow, I find solace in Dolph's presence. A flicker of hope eases the pain. This feels right, even if I don't understand any of it. I blink back the tears.

"Thank you, Dolph. I'm glad you'll be here when I return."

I squeeze his hand and lean back against the pillow.

The doctor and nurse release the brakes on the bed and roll me from the room.

A glance over my shoulder reveals Dolph watching me. Hope flickers in his topaz eyes.

And it brightens as the doctor and nurse roll me back to my room over an hour later. I'm exhausted from the battery of tests and hungry. Just as we reach the door where Dolph stands by his cot, a growl fills the air. His eyes widen and drop to my belly. The palm of my good hand slaps onto my roiling belly. I giggle, and he scowls.

"Doc, you removed the nutrients drip but didn't give her any food? Not good," he says as he grabs a radio from the floor. He barks orders for a variety of foods as he follows us into the room. He ends the call. "How is she?"

"All tests show improvements, as expected. Still a bit of swelling on the brain and tenderness in the broken areas. Otherwise, the coma and her natural healing helped. We'll continue to monitor her here. I'll call Alpha now. Jane, eat small portions then rest. We'll see you in the morning."

They leave the room.

"Jane? Do you remember your name?"

"No. I figured Jane Doe's better than What's Her Name," I respond then mutter. "Or *Princess.*"

He smiles with me at my humor attempt in a messed-up situation.

"Seems like I'll be here for a while. You might as well pull up a chair and tell me about yourself," I say.

Dolph grins and carries a chair to the side of my bed. He tells me all about Viking wolf shifters, his puphood with his best friends, and the New York Wolves Pack. He's not forthcoming with details on his military career but tells me about his roles as pack beta and COO of Moen, Inc. He talks through dinner and until my eyes droop.

"Okay, that's enough for tonight. You had a long day. Now that you've eaten, it's time for bed, Baby Girl," he says as he rises from the chair.

My lips quirk as I recall his request to use the endearment instead of the Jane pseudonym. My body heated with memories of the erotic dreams as he groaned *Baby Girl* with his orgasms. I couldn't possibly deny him.

"Or are you being a Naughty Girl with naughty thoughts running in your mind?" He asks with a sexy smirk.

I duck my head as my cheeks flame.

He places the calloused pad of his thumb beneath my chin to lift my head. Our eyes meet. Lust smolders in his hooded gaze. It scorches a trail over my cheeks and down to my lips. He groans when the tip of my tongue darts out to moisten my lower lip. His thumb brushes across it then pulls it down. His eyes fixate on my mouth.

Drawn to him, I lean forward, my eyes focused on his full lips. They part on a hiss. He pinches my chin to halt my movement. My eyes fly up to his. They're molten gold. But he blinks and shakes his head.

"As much as I want to not only devour that sweet mouth of yours and pound you into this mattress, you need to sleep. I never start something I can't finish to full satisfaction. Come, bathroom then bed."

Not the way I envisioned coming. But I nod and swing my legs off the bed.

"Nope. I've got you, Baby Girl."

He insists on carrying me to and from the bathroom, even though Doc confirmed I can bear weight on my ankle. I don't mind since his comforting scent engulfs me. Once he tucks me in bed, I fall fast asleep.

No erotic dreams tonight.

Instead, a pack of wolves dominates my sleep. They frolic and howl in the moonlight. Their song blends with the crashing of waves on the sandy shore. The ocean breeze carries the crispness of saltwater as it ruffles their fur.

Three massive wolves—black, golden, and tawny—

stand on a bluff staring at the ocean in the distance. Their flashing eyes scan the empty horizon. As one, they throw their heads back and howl.

Pain pierces my heart, and tears slip from my closed eyes at their mournful cry.

igny

"Hey. How do you feel this morning?"

I watch Garrett stride into my room. The muscles of his long, thick legs flex beneath the black cargo pants with each step of his heavy combat boots. My eyes linger on the bulge at his crotch. I blink, surprised to see it increase in size at my gaze. If the erotic dreams are real, then he's packing an impressive cock.

My pussy spasms at the memory of him drilling me into a bed as I screamed his name until my voice croaked. I squirm to relieve the building pressure at the apex of my thighs. But the cotton gown abrades my pebbled nipples. The instant jolt to my pussy forces me to tug my lower lip between my teeth to bite back the unexpected moan. *Gah!* What these men—or wolves—do to me.

And to think more exist outside of their pack, including the one they say I must come from. I just wish I knew it and the others. I'm certain a familiar face would trigger my memories. Once the blizzard ends, I'll have to go somewhere. I can't stay here. Or with the three men.

They may be sexy as all sin and claim to be my fated mates—well, at least Dolph and Garrett do—but it can't possibly work. Three to one? I mean, the sex would be explosive based on the erotic dreams. But that's not enough to *bond* myself to all three forever. I may not have all my memories. But that's a weird situation—human or wolf shifter.

Do we live in the same house? Share one enormous bed? Have foursomes every time we fuck? Oh, and what about children, I mean pups? How would we determine who's the daddy? Constant DNA tests? Not to mention they may be best friends, but they certainly bicker. At least, over or about me. I don't want to come between them and ruin their lifelong friendship. There's no way it could work, and would I allow it to? What a hot mess.

The desire thrumming through me evaporates. I sigh and shake my head.

"I hope that's not your answer."

I blink at Garrett's voice.

Talk about zoning out. I refocus my eyes to find him at the foot of my bed with his head cocked. His eyebrows dip as he studies my face. Even frowning, the man is handsome. The slight crinkles between his brows and around his eyes add to his sex appeal. I doubt anything can detract from his masculine beauty. *Sigh.*

"No, not at all. My mind was in another place," I say, then snort. "Yeah, it definitely is since I can't remember anything aside from—"

I bite my lip as my cheeks heat. No way do I want him thinking all I do is relive the dreams. *Gah!*

He chuckles and drops a bundle on the bed.

"Stop overthinking. The more you stress, the less you'll allow your mind to heal. You're safe here, fed, and clothed," he says and gestures to the bundle. "I brought some clothes for you, long-sleeved Henleys, cargo pants, joggers, and socks. We keep a fresh supply for the enforcers. I skipped the boots since your ankle still has the soft cast."

I scoot forward and sort through the items. Now, I cock my head and peer at him from beneath the long fringe of my eyelashes.

"Did you skip the bras and panties on purpose, too?" I ask in a voice that surprises me with its sultriness. "You want to envision me naked beneath these baggy clothes?"

I refuse to look away even as my cheeks burn. It's time I get a rile out of Mr. Cool, aside from his flashing eyes.

I get those and more. His molars grind, and he fists the footboard until his knuckles turn white. Breaths saw in and out of his flared nostrils. His Adam's apple bobs up and down his throat where tendons stand out in bas-relief. A low growl emerges from his heaving chest.

I watch mesmerized as his features waver between

those of a human and a wolf. Forehead widens. Nose elongates to form a blocky snout. Teeth lengthen to sharp fangs. And of course, his eyes flash electric blue. His body increases in mass. His muscles gaining more muscles. The room fills with the crackling of bones and ligaments. The metal bed frame creaks from his iron grip.

Oh my.

He closes his eyes and inhales deeply. During continued controlled breathing, his body returns to its normal yet still large size. His eyes open and lock with mine.

"Careful, Princess, you taunt a beast clinging to the edge. Let's keep to the topic of your healing. Understand?"

"No."

His head snaps back as though I slapped him. He lowers it, and his eyes narrow.

"*No?*"

"No."

"Really? What part do you not understand?"

I scoot further down the bed and rise to my knees, careful of my ankle. As I stare into his eyes, I lift my hand to his face. He stares at me while my fingertips trail along his eyebrows, along his cheekbone, and across his mouth. His eyes close as a puff of air caresses my fingers. A humming sound emerges from the back of his throat.

"I don't understand any of this," I respond as I continue to trace the contours of his face. He leans into my touches as I continue. "Why do I have a deep-rooted attraction to the three of you? It reaches my soul. What makes you so sure our destinies intertwine? I don't know you, and what if I have a lover?"

His eyes open to slits on a possessive growl.

I shake my head as I place my fingertips against his mouth.

"How could it work when the three of you argue about me? I don't want to come between best friends. Plus, Colin hates me. Most of all, how can I be a wolf shifter? I don't sense a beast's presence within me."

My fingers slip from his mouth to allow him to answer my questions.

"Tell me, Garrett. I need to have something solid about my life," I whisper as tears blur my vision.

I didn't expect to get emotional. But the whole memory loss scares me. If I can't remember anything and return to my past life, I need to know if my future lies with them.

In an instant, Garrett scoops me into his arms and sits on the bed. One hand presses against my hip to meld me to his rumbling chest, while the other hand cups my face. I keep my eyes lowered, embarrassed by my emotional outburst, but he's not having it. He tilts my head until our eyes connect. Concern darkens his glacial eyes to cobalt. I tremble at the intensity.

"Never hide yourself from us or be embarrassed. You mean everything to us with your happiness of the utmost importance—"

"Not to Colin. He hates me. Wants nothing to do with me—"

"He can be an ass. But he doesn't hate you. He doesn't

believe in fated mates. It's his story to tell. So, his reaction to you caught him off guard. He spent plenty of hours watching over you. Don't let his snarky behavior fool you. Trust me."

"How can I trust you when I know so little about you and any of this. Last night, Dolph told me about himself and mentioned things about you and Colin. Help me understand, Garrett. Answer my questions. Please."

Garrett

MY CHEST CONSTRICTS at her questions—or Jane, as Dolph tells us the name she chose. Even that broke my heart. To not remember her actual name and to choose one used for an unknown female must upset her. And whatever upsets her, stabs the three of us in the chest with a silver ice pick. Excruciating since aside from being her lovers—as the dreams prove—our roles are her protectors, caregivers, and providers. We're hardwired for our fated mate's happiness.

Even though I won't go forward with the bond for her safety, I will tend to her needs. Despite my dick's disapproval, I won't fuck her either. The risk of losing control to my wolf in his desire to issue the claiming bite would prove too hard, even for me. Both of us will have to make do with self-satisfaction. Already, the muscles in my right arm grow bigger than the left, thanks to the nightly dreams of her. Oh, well.

But she won't miss out. Dolph can barely contain himself. I sense the rise in his desire to claim her, especially now that she's awake. If he's not at her bedside or on his cot, he stomps around pissed he's separated from her. This morning, I laid into his ass when he grumbled in response to training duty. With the blizzard still raging, the enforcers need more drills time indoors, and it's his responsibility to manage them. He literally snarled when I told him I'd check on Jane. I shut that shit down with a blast of Alpha command. His ass is in the gym right now.

The interaction proves Jane's concern about the three of us arguing about her. From what I know, multiple mates get along with the focus on the she-wolf since the males set aside their issues to make it all about her. I don't know the males' rankings in their packs. But with us being Alpha, beta, and lead enforcer, who are Alpha males, it may prove impossible.

Then again, it doesn't matter since I won't bond with Jane. I'll add the role of referee if Dolph and Colin go at each other's throats. Despite what she thinks, Colin wants her. The ass is too much of an alphahole to admit it. Her *beast* comment didn't help with his already on-the-fence mindset. Undoubtedly, he'll get over it. Her pull is strong.

I sensed it the minute I entered her room. Like Janet Jackson sings about a moth to a flame, Jane drew me in. But will I burn? Or will I cause her to?

As she sat in bed and watched me walk in, her eyes

swept over me, like her unique scent. Pure passion poured from her heated gaze. And when it lingered on my cock, the fucker nearly punched a hole in my cargo pants. I could've walked on three legs to reach her bed.

Then she went all vixen on me, and I teetered between man and wolf. The bastard reared up in a millisecond. I had to wrestle control back. He snarled as he slunk back to the fringes of my mind.

He may have been tamed. But my erection only deflated when her beautiful eyes filled with tears. She gutted me.

Now, with her in my arms, I rumble to soothe her and ache to pull her beneath me to drive away all pain with same cock. Instead of tears of sadness, I'd have her crying from absolute bliss. She'd forget but not her memory. The pleasure would erase the pain, one orgasm at a time, until she begged me for no more. And I'd give her a few to ensure I chased the pain away for good.

However, that's not what she needs right now. She asks for answers, and I'll do as I'm hardwired and give her what she needs.

But first, I bury my face in her hair and inhale her unique scent mixed with the fresh scent of her shampoo. A calmness like I've never known before Jane washes over me. Talk about absolute bliss. One last whiff, and I straighten and look into her eyes.

"The soul-reaching attraction is the natural bond fated mates sense with one another. The connection only you share. It will grow stronger after the male wolf shifter issues the claiming bite to the she-wolf. The bond will then be complete and unbreakable. Only death can sever it. If the she-wolf dies before the male, he will follow her into the afterlife unable to bear being apart from his other half. If the male succumbs first, the female will grieve. But she may live to find another mate."

I pause for Jane to absorb my explanation.

She glances over my shoulder as she contemplates my words.

My thumb strokes the curve of her hip. I can't stop the urge to touch her, preferably skin on skin. It pleases my wolf—and I must admit me too—she doesn't shy away. Instead, she unconsciously shimmies her hips.

It takes another full rein on my control to keep my cock flaccid. It wouldn't do to scare her with the true beast and have her leaping from my lap. My thoughts turn to Blaise's techie. I bet he'll give in a couple more days. Or else Colin will flay his back. The grisly image works. The beast recoils.

"I see. What happens if they don't complete the bond?"

My wolf growls low. I ignore him.

"The female will sense a loss. However, the male could go feral and either die or be put down if the pack believes he's a danger."

Her eyes widen as her mouth forms a perfect O.

Yeah, tell me about it. It'll take a toll on me. But I will survive it. I must. As the Alpha of my pack, I cannot lose my shit. My responsibility lies with them, second to my fated mate. I'll find a way to make both work without me claiming her.

"That's terrible," she whispers then glances away. She continues as though speaking to herself. "That could change things."

My wolf leaps to his feet with a toothy grin, happy to hear she cares. Yeah, a twinge got me too. Instead of responding, I go on to her next question.

"Aside from your unique scent being on our first breath when we were born and our wolves recognizing yours, the gods wouldn't make us react to you. That's the destiny part. We know one another at the cellular level. The dormant connection bursts to the forefront once mates encounter one another. In time, they get to know each other."

I raise an eyebrow and all but snarl the rest.

"As for you having a lover, that's over, full stop."

This time, her eyes narrow and flash silver—and she thinks her wolf doesn't exist.

"Seriously?! Not one of you can tell me what to do, Garrett. Don't let this fated mate stuff go to your heads," she says then glances down. "Either one!"

My arms tighten around her as she squirms to get off my lap. Guess she felt the beast after all. Even flaccid, he's an anaconda.

"That's me soft, Princess. But if you keep wiggling that ass of yours, you'll rouse the beast to his full capacity," I say, then chuckle as she huffs. "I will answer truthfully, always. Now, be still, or I'll spank said ass."

She gasps, affronted. However, the musky aroma of her arousal rises from beneath the thin cotton gown. My mouth waters. My wolf sniffs the air. She stills.

"Good girl. I am the Alpha of the pack. Dolph, Colin, and I are alpha males. As their leader, they obey my commands. As best friends, we vie for dominance. Disagreements happen. However, we love and respect each other and do not hold grudges. They would die for me as I would for them. Our bond is strong."

She sags in relief.

"Good, because you have history together. I'm the outsider," she says sadly.

My wolf and I bristle.

"No!" I bark, and she jumps. I rub her leg and continue. "Sorry, Princess. I didn't mean to startle you."

She responds with a meek smile and a shrug without looking at me.

Unh-uh.

I grasp her chin between my thumb and forefinger to align our gazes. She flutters her eyelids. I cock an eyebrow and continue.

"You are not an outsider. The gods brought you to us. Hell, I wouldn't put it past them being the cause of this non-ending blizzard. It's a crazy way to bring you into our lives with the crash and forced proximity. But things happen for reasons unbeknownst to us. We accept them as gifts from the gods."

As I speak the last part, my wolf cocks an eyebrow—if wolves could—as if to say, look who's talking?

I guess it's a bit hypocritical since I'm fighting the urge to mate Jane. Hell, I can't call her that. She's Princess. A much more appropriate moniker since she's destined to be our Queen. The Luna of the New York Wolves Pack. If I—as the Alpha—claim her.

I close my eyes and groan in frustration.

"I highly doubt Colin views me as a gift from the gods."

Her words draw me from my musings.

Good distraction.

"He'll come around."

My wolf snorts as if to ask, will you?

I ignore him and continue my focus on Princess. As she continues to sit on my lap, I answer her questions about me. Once she's satisfied, I tell her about growing up as a wolf shifter in a pack then following my father as pack Alpha and CEO of Moen, Inc. Our conversation flows easily. I don't fail to notice how comfortable we are in each other's presence. So much so, I grouse when I get a call over the radio to join Colin in the dungeons.

"Well, duty calls. If you need anything, press one on the phone to reach me. Otherwise, lunch will arrive here soon, and I'm sure Dolph will show up later on. Get some rest for now."

I lift her from my lap and place her on the bed. She smiles up at me.

"Thank you, Garrett. I feel better knowing more about you and what's going on with the four of us. It's a lot to take in. But for whatever reason, I trust you."

She lifts her shoulders and bites her lower lip.

My fingers itch to free the plump flesh and slant my mouth over hers. Instead, I nod, not trusting my words won't come out gruffly. Then I pivot on my heel and stride for the door. I dare not glance back at her for fear I'll take her right then and there.

Once in the hallway, I exhale the breath I didn't realize I held. *Keep it together, Garrett!*

If only it were so easy.

CHAPTER 13

 igny

"Here's a pad and pen so you can write anything that comes to mind. Doc also suggests music can trigger memories. I created some playlists for you on an iPod I scrounged up. Did you finish dinner? Eating right counts, too."

As Garrett predicted, Dolph enters my room in the early evening. I grin as he rattles on.

Who would expect a big guy like him to be such a softie with me? It's only been over a day I since I woke up, and he's spent most of his time with me. Of the three, he's the one who's resolute about me being his fated mate. He speaks as though I agreed to the reverse harem.

On the other hand, Colin makes good on his word and

hasn't been around since he stormed out of my room. Recalling his harsh reaction hurts anew.

"Hey, what's wrong, Baby Girl?"

Dolph's gentle voice interrupts the sting. He cups my cheek and brushes his thumb along my face. My eyes close on a sigh as I lean into his comfort.

"I can only imagine how hard it must be for you. And sadly, there's no way to guarantee your memory will return," he pauses at my sob and presses his lips to the crown of my head. "However, you have the three of us. You're not alone and won't have to deal with this situation by yourself. We'll take care of you, Baby Girl."

He scoops me from the bed and sits with me between his legs. His front presses against my back as he leans forward to pull the items he brought onto my lap.

"Let's get some music going. Put one in your ear, and I'll do the same with the other one. We can listen together. Make notes on the pad about whatever comes to mind."

I slip the earbud in, and he starts a playlist titled *Dance Time*. He picked good songs I bop to until he groans. I pull the earbud out and peer over my shoulder at him.

His eyebrows furrow over eyes squeezed shut. The back of his head rests on the pillows propped against the headboard.

"What's wrong?"

"You're killing me, Baby Girl."

I frown and shift around to face him fully.

"What do you mean? How?"

Dolph opens his eyes partially and stares at me.

"You're wiggling your ass, babe," he groans, then leans forward until we're nose-to-nose. "Right. Against. My. Dick."

"Oh!" I exclaim and shuffle away. But he grabs my hips and pulls me back to him. "But—"

"I'd rather fuck you into the bed. But I'll settle for a little bump and grind as you dance. Just don't blame me if I blow my load."

He narrows his eyes as I giggle.

"Not funny, babe. Not funny at all. I haven't lost my shit since I was a pup. It happened when I came across a couple going at it hard in the woods and couldn't tear my eyes away. I almost busted a nut when the she-wolf winked at me. You see, wolf shifters are pretty sexual. We view intimacy as a daily necessity. She didn't care I watched them. In fact, she made a show of it as she bounced on his cock and stared over his shoulder at me. He came, and so did I."

I laugh even harder with unladylike snorts.

Dolph twists his lips to the side.

I laugh more until he tickles me.

"I'll give you something to laugh about."

He's relentless. Fingers catch me under my good arm, along my waist, and even at my neck. I wiggle and laugh until I'm breathless.

"G—Give... Give!"

He chuckles wickedly and continues despite my pleas.

Somehow, I'm on my back with him on his haunches between my legs. He stares down at me. The hospital gown bunches around my hips where the tips of his fingers slip beneath to tickle my waist. Eyes closed, my head thrashes as my fingers grasp his forearm. When my hips buck, he growls. My eyes pop open.

His eyes glow from an internal furnace with his wolf close to the surface. They narrow as his scorching gaze drips molten gold from my face, over my breasts, and down to the apex of my thighs. He locks in on my private spot. His chest rises and falls with a feral growl.

The abrupt change from playfulness to carnality morphs my laughter to moans. My pussy softens. Juices gather from the depths of my core. They slicken my inner walls and dribble to the exposed edges of my pussy lips. It's only then I noticed the cool air on my heated flesh.

Dolph inhales audibly.

My gaze jumps to his face.

It's distorted with the shape of his wolf. He stares back at me with an expression full of sensuality, possessiveness, fierceness.

I moan. My back bows as my nipples bead. Instead of pushing him away, my fingers dig into the corded muscles of his forearm to drag him closer. Every cell in my body hums to have this male pressed to me.

"Dolph," I mewl as I stare up at him through heavy lidded eyes.

"I've got you, Baby Girl," he says in a ragged breath.

He keeps his eyes on mine as he lowers his chest. I scoonch towards the foot of the bed to give him more room. He growls in approval as his big body rests on the bed between my spread thighs. His hands push the gown higher.

I gasp as more cool air caresses my lower half. My pussy constricts, drawing the exposed lower lips inward.

Dolph hisses.

My body levitates as the flat of his tongue laves my wet seam. I cry out in ecstasy.

He grunts and lifts my legs onto his broad shoulders. His arms wrap around the outside of my thighs for his hands to hold me in place. I suck in a breath when his fingers splay my pussy lips. It comes out in a strangled cry as his nose nuzzles me. He breathes in deeply and groans. Fingers press into the soft flesh of my inner thighs.

I moan his name as my fingernails claw the cover.

"So sweet, Baby Girl," he growls against my slick pussy. He places a kiss on the lower lips before the tip of his tongue probes the entrance. "Mmmm… Delicious."

He slides in slowly, savoring the juices. His tongue laps at my inner walls to catch every drop. But more gushes from my core. He grunts and groans in carnal appreciation as he makes a meal out of my pussy. The wet sounds fill the air, blooming with the fragrance of my arousal.

My back arcs, pressing my shoulders into the mattress when his tongue strokes my G-spot. Electricity radiates from the sensitive area hidden on my upper wall. It spreads from my curled toes to my clenched ass ending at my scalp. A full-body shudder takes hold of me as I climax with a wordless cry.

"Keep cumming for me."

Dolph's guttural command reaches me through a fog of rapture.

Frissons from the aftershock course through me. My limbs twitch with each passing wave. But he gives me not a moment to bask in post-orgasmic bliss.

His tongue curls around my engorged clit and sucks. Hard. My hips strain against the hold he has on my thighs, desperate to ride his face to another mind-blowing climax. But he growls around my clit and nips at the sensitive bundle of nerves. I yelp.

Seconds later, he laves the pain away. But it adds fuel to the locomotive barreling down my spine.

"Oh, Dolph… Dolph… Please!"

"Cum for me again, Baby Girl!"

His roar increases the speed, and the orgasm hits me full force.

I scream incoherently as my body locks up. Only my pussy pulsates as it repeatedly clamps down on his tongue spearing through my folds. The tip hits my G-spot again and again. The erotic pleasure rolls through me—a never-ending freight train without breaks.

His fingers dig into my thighs as he gulps my juices. Another orgasm follows. I beg for him to stop. He shakes his head, mouth pressed to my pussy, and grunts for one more. My body obeys his command while my mind drifts.

The mattress dips as Dolph crawls up my body. Along the way, he plants kisses on my belly, the pointed tips of my nipples, and on the side of my neck. At the juncture where it meets my shoulder, he lingers.

His warm breath pants on my sweat-soaked skin. I shiver at the contact. He inhales and lets the breath skitter over my skin before he planks above me. His hooded eyes lock on mine.

"Dolph," I murmur in a blissful daze.

His eyes drop to my parted lips. On a groan, he slants his over them. His tongue plunges inside and sweeps around. He moans when my tongue tangles with his.

The musky taste of my juices coats his tongue. I lap at it, enthralled.

He cups the back of my head to control the kiss. I moan and give in to his dominance.

"Mine! You. Are. Mine!"

Even as my body basks in the afterglow of his passion, my mind holds back.

Am I?

DOLPH

WITH ONE LAST look at her peacefully sleeping form, I close the door behind me as I leave the room. I pause at my cot but shake my head. No way can I sleep now. I'm too keyed up and my cock drips with pre-cum. At least I didn't blow my load after all. I grunt and adjust the heavy length that tents my joggers.

My head snaps up at the sound of someone approaching.

The nurse turns the corner. She smiles.

"Hi, beta. How's Jane?"

I grumble at the name, irritated it's a reminder she doesn't know who she is. But at the same time, if she knew her name, she'd know who she is and whether she has a male in her life. The idea of another enjoying her body as I did makes my wolf and me snarl and gnash our teeth. I don't give a damn what Garrett says. Baby Girl stays with us. She's ours.

"Uh, Dolph? Are you all right?"

The cautious voice of the nurse snaps me out of the red haze.

As pack beta, the unmated she-wolves are my responsibility. So, I don't want to upset her. I shake my head to clear it and nod.

"Yes, just thinking about something," I say with an attempt at a smile.

She raises both eyebrows and nods slowly as her lips curl up.

"Whatever it was, I'm glad I'm not on the receiving end!" She quips, then gestures at the door. "Is she awake? I want to check her vitals."

Knowing she's worn out from the multiple orgasms, I don't want her disturbed.

"No, she's asleep. Long day and all. Better to let her rest unless it's absolutely necessary."

The nurse's eyes flick between me and the door. Her

nostrils flare slightly, then realization dawns in her hazel eyes. She nods. Brown eyes twinkle with quirked lips.

"Gotcha. The readings would be off, anyway. Well, I'll be at the nurse's station overnight. Feel free to handle your business."

She adds the last with a pointed stare at my crotch. Then she pivots on her heel with a giggle.

I grip the back of my neck and stretch. Naturally, she scented Baby Girl all over me. The obvious boner I'm sporting didn't help. Ah, well. We're sexual creatures, after all.

With no interest in the bed and needing to put space between my fated mate and me before I go back in and finish the deal, I stride from the hospital. I have another source of relief.

"Hey, you up for a lifting session?"

"This late?"

I snicker at Colin's surly response over the radio.

"It's only eight. Or are you already asleep, gramps?"

He growls.

"You better hope I don't let the bar drop on your throat, fucker."

I make my way to the gym. Not surprisingly, others workout at the various stations or on the mats. A bump to my shoulder follows Colin striding past me. Then he stiffens and stalks back towards me with slitted eyes. He doesn't hide the fact he sniffs me when he moves into my personal space. Stepping back, he snarls.

"So, you popped that cherry?"

Anger blazes through me. I throw an elbow to his throat. But he blocks it. We punch, jab, and kick our way further in to the gym. Others stop at the sound of our angry snarls. I ignore their stares as I concentrate on kicking Colin's ass for disrespecting our mate.

His eyes drill into mine unblinkingly. Equally matched, he gives as good as I dish out. It's a fight of titans. And I'm not letting up.

No one, and I mean no one, speaks ill of her. As rude as his ass was when he stalked out of her room, he's lucky I didn't get him then. I understand he doesn't believe in fated mates and the unexpected situation surprised him. But fuck that now.

Ask stupid questions, get smart answers.

He swipes out with his legs and catches my ankles. I drop but backflip up. My wolf scratches beneath the surface to break free. But I rein him in. It won't come to our wolves facing off. We'll handle this man-to-man.

So instead of lifting weights, we fight weaving around the equipment. The others move as we cut a swath through in an irregular path. Fists connect with faces. Legs and feet smash flanks. We go all out.

"What the fuck?!"

Garrett's voice booms in the massive space.

"Stop. Right. Now."

His Alpha command hits harder than an overhand punch to the temple.

Colin and I stagger then drop. We glare at each other as our chests heave.

"Hallway. Now."

Garrett spins and marches towards the doors without waiting for us to acknowledge his directive. He knows we cannot disobey our Alpha.

I leap to my feet and stalk after him. Colin keeps his distance. The others watch but remain silent. Tension increases tenfold. Great.

At the end of the hallway, Garrett stands with his fists on his hips and feet planted apart. Thunderous glacial blue eyes spark with lightning at the presence of his wolf. He pins us with balls-withering glares as we approach.

We stand at attention before him with our arms at our sides, heads up, but gazes lowered in deference to him being our Alpha. Right now, he's not Garrett our best friend, he's all pack leader. And a totally pissed-off one.

We're screwed.

Silence stretches on while he racks us with sharp glares. One whiff lets us know he's battling to keep his wolf at bay. I know if the arousal scent of Baby Girl on me riled Colin —who claims to care less—then it damn sure set Garrett precariously on the edge.

I guess I could blame myself. I sort of flaunted the intimacy I shared with her. It's only natural for them and their wolves to react to her scent on another male. Even more so since none of us claimed her. Yet.

But my admission doesn't mean Colin can get away with being disrespectful. He better watch his mouth, or this won't be the last time I—

"Did you have sex with her?"

Garrett's blunt question catches me off guard.

My eyes snap to his. His growl comes from deep within his chest. I lower my gaze hurriedly.

"No, Alpha."

He inhales sharply.

"What did you do?"

"Oral."

"You on her, or vice versa, or both?"

If he weren't my Alpha, I'd bristle at the level of detail. Instead, I answer she was the recipient. He's silent then speaks to Colin.

"Who threw the first punch?"

"Dolph."

"What did you do?"

He knows Colin is the hothead of us and would be the one to trigger me to react.

"I asked if he popped her cherry."

Bones crackle. But not from Garrett shifting to his wolf. He stretches his neck in an effort to calm himself. He's an outstanding leader, not easily riled. But a fated mate can mess up even the most controlled male.

"You do realize the inappropriateness of your question?"

"Yes, Alpha. If I may, Alpha?"

"Yes."

"Dolph should be more respectful of the she-wolf. He left her and entered a room full of males who would detect her arousal on him. If he didn't want a comment, he should have showered or gone to his rooms."

I bite back a growl at his audacity to flip this shit on me.

"True. However, your question was crass," Garrett turns to me. "And you should maintain better control over your-self. You struck when you should have had a discussion with the male who's also her fated mate. Both of you are out of order."

"Yes, Alpha," Colin and I respond.

"At ease," Garrett says then sighs. "Walk with me, guys."

We fall in step with our best friend and head away from the gym.

"The gods destined the she-wolf to be our fated mate. She may not have her memories as a wolf shifter. But she is. She also doesn't know if she has a male in her life. Which adds to the situation. So, I stand by what I said before. I will not allow either of you to claim her until she knows more."

"What about you?"

He pauses and turns to me.

"I'm not claiming her. Our missions put her at risk. However, I will assure I meet her needs, except for one. I won't have sex with her."

Talk about mic drop.

Garrett shrugs at my reaction.

"Well, I'm not claiming her either."

We turn to Colin, who shakes his head.

"I don't want a mate, fated or not," he says then smirks at me. "She's all yours, bro. Just don't get your panties in a bunch again."

I narrow my eyes.

Garrett chuckles.

"You never let up, do you?"

Colin shrugs.

"You know me. Can't stop. Won't stop."

I shake my head at both of them.

"Stop fooling yourselves. You cannot ignore the fated mate bond. And I have no interest in putting down my best friends. When you get over yourselves, let's talk about how we'll make it work. We can't keep fighting. She's the center of this foursome. Her happiness is of the utmost importance. Think about that, you fuckers. Good night!"

I jog away, leaving them gaping. At least I got a good workout in.

Now, let's see what tomorrow brings.

CHAPTER 14

igny

"YOU'RE DOING MUCH BETTER despite the bruising still on your face and elsewhere, Jane. Don't let that bother you. More important, the tests results show improvement. Now, let's check your ankle and arm. It's probable you healed enough to remove the casts."

"Thank you, Doc. I feel stronger than when I first woke up. I guess a few days of good food and interactions with others help."

My cheeks blush at the memory of Dolph eating me out like a starved man. The way his skilled tongue worked with his deft fingers to bring me to countless orgasms heats me from my core out. Pinned to the bed by his big body, unable to stop his carnal assault, drove me over each time. Just his groans and demands made my pussy spasm uncontrollably.

Then the kiss. Oh. My. Goodness. Talk about breathtaking. I pant, just reliving his tongue dominating my mouth. And the taste of my juices. Whoa.

I shift on the examination table as my pussy throbs with need.

Doc's polite cough pulls me from my musings.

I refocus on the room to find his nostrils flared as he sits on a stool next to my feet. My cheeks flame when I realize he must detect my arousal. A titter draws my attention to the nurse. Her brown cheeks tinge pink as she holds back laughter. She must sense it, too.

Oops. I have to be aware of my body's reactions around wolf shifters.

"Ready?"

I close my eyes at Doc's question. Not in preparation of the removal of the cast. Rather in embarrassment. I take a deep breath and open my eyes as I nod on the exhalation.

"Ready."

He removes the ankle cast and instructs me to point, flex, then to walk in new sneakers. I marvel at how the break healed so quickly. I doubt a human would recover from a broken ankle in such a brief span of time.

The same applies to my arm. Smooth skin and set straight. The only sign of an issue is a bit of stiffness. Doc assures me it's from being held in one position for over a week.

He gives me a list of exercises to strengthen and to stretch the muscles of my arm and my ankle and recommends I walk three times a day. He tells me I should use the long hallway outside the infirmary for an uninterrupted path.

As we walk to the infirmary entrance, I ponder if perhaps there's some merit to them saying I'm a she-wolf. I can think of a number of reasons I—or any other woman— would lust after the three men. But the quick healing? Not so easy to justify.

"Doc! We're coming in hot with the techie. Be there in five."

Colin's voice comes through the radio on Doc's belt.

He turns to the nurse and gives her instructions then faces me.

"Jane, you can walk along the hallway. But when Colin arrives, stand to the side and face the wall. Do not engage with anyone," he says urgently as he glances down the hallway. "And don't overexert yourself. Any pain, elevate your limb and apply an ice pack from the refrigerator in your room. Understood?"

I nod, and he hustles to the infirmary.

What the hell does that mean?

My gaze shifts to the opposite direction at the clomping of combat boots on the tile. Colin leads two others with a third carried between them. His head hangs with his arms draped over the men's shoulders.

I freeze as Colin's eyes lock on me. His tawny eyebrows

dip. But he says nothing. His frown reminds me to face the wall. Hurriedly, I spin and duck my head.

As the men rush by, the injured man lifts his head. His black eyes focus on me. He tilts his head and sniffs. Busted lips curve into a bloody toothless grin.

I gasp.

Colin jerks around. His eyes flick from me to the man—who drops his head—but not before he smirks at me.

"Watch yourself, fucker," Colin snarls as he cuffs the man upside the head. "Take him inside. I'll be right there."

Not wanting Colin's ire, I yank my head around to face the wall. I hold my breath as I hear him stalk up behind me. His warm breath fans across the shell of my ear as he bends down.

"Oh, *Princess*, I'm sure Doc told you to not engage. But you didn't listen. Did you, Naughty Girl?"

I shudder and not in fright. I mutter a curse as my nipples pebble and my pussy softens. My fists clench, trying to ward off my carnal reaction to the sexy as sin alphahole. And to will away my arousal. No way do I want him to get an inkling of my interest in him.

But I fail.

He inhales along the curve of my neck and chuckles wickedly.

"No-go, *Princess*. I'm not your boy toy Dolph."

He spins on his heel and jogs into the infirmary.

A growl slips past my clenched teeth.

Damn that man, wolf shifter, jerk!

My body vibrates.

Rather than being anywhere near him by returning to my room, I walk down the hallway in the direction he came from. My goal to get as far away as possible from him. Even if he makes me hot and bothered. Those fierce amber eyes and soft, full lips. So, what if they narrow and curl up in a sneer? *Gah!*

Without realizing it, I've walked quite a bit from the infirmary. I glance over my shoulder at the distance I traveled. Doc is right. The long hallway proves perfect for my walk. Deciding I've gone far enough, I turn back.

Better to be in my room when Colin leaves the infirmary than to bump into him in the hallway. Despite it being wide enough for four people to pass, his bigger-than-life presence dwarfs the space.

My mind goes back to him close behind me. Mere centimeters separated us. The heat of his body burning my back. The warmth of his breath tickling my ear. A tremble shudders through me, and I wrap my arms around my waist.

"What are you doing out here?"

I startle with a squeal then whip my head around to find Garrett behind me.

"My apologies, Princess," he says in a tone so different from Colin. "Does Doc know you're in the hallway this far from the infirmary?"

"Yes. He removed the casts and told me to walk the hallway for exercise," I respond as I lift my arm and tap my foot. "A little stiff and weak, but all healed. See?"

I have the urge to seek praise from this commanding

man. My core warms at the panty-melting smile he graces me with.

"Excellent news," he says as his glacial blue eyes glide up my body to my face. "You look good, Princess."

I preen.

He grins and scoops me into a bridal carry.

"But I think you've done enough for today. Besides, I need to get to the infirmary quickly, and I don't want you rushing on that ankle."

Instead of protesting, I loop my arm around his broad shoulders and press my cheek to his chest. The rhythmic beat of his heart soothes me. The enticing blend of sandalwood and vanilla fills my nose. I inhale deeply and sigh. I could stay in Garrett's powerful arms all day.

"Comfortable, Princess?" He says in a low, raspy voice. A steady rumble vibrates through his chest to wrap around my body.

"Mmhmm," I purr and burrow deeper as peace settles over me.

A soft pillow replaces Garrett's firm pec, and my eyes open. I glance around. How in the world did I fall asleep in a matter of minutes? I sit up. But he shakes his head.

"There's someone in the infirmary I want you to stay away from. Do not leave your room. Understand?"

"Yes, Alpha," I respond, knowing he likes to hear me address him in that manner.

As expected, his eyes deepen to cobalt blue. But he blinks and the glacial color returns. He removes my sneakers and places the cover over me.

"Now, get some rest. As always, if you need me, press one on the phone."

"Yes, Alpha," I repeat.

"Good girl."

My chest warms. And pussy, if I'm being honest.

He smirks and strides from the room.

I watch his ass flex beneath his cargo pants, then pull the cover up to my eyes when he glances over his shoulder and busts me.

"Rest," he commands with a chuckle as he shuts the door.

I watch him through the window head further into the infirmary. I guess the injured man must be there. As my eyes drift closed, I wonder what happened to his teeth.

Garrett

OUTSIDE OF HER ROOM, I adjust my erect cock as I head towards the operating room. I inhale deeply to draw her unique scent into every cell of my body. Damn. It gets harder each time to fight the urge to claim her. She just feels so right in my arms. I never want to let her go.

But as I round the corner, I see Colin outside the OR where Blaise's techie is on the table.

No way can I expose her to this side of my life.

But there's more to what you do. Moen, Inc. Life on Moen Island. Spoil her with all your billions can buy.

"Doc says he'll be fine."

Colin cuts into my inner voice. Thankfully. I need to remain focused.

"Good. The replacement of his teeth with silver implants wasn't the smartest idea. We need him to have the ability to speak. Right?"

Colin shrugs and glances over my shoulder. His nostrils flare.

Here we go. But I raise my hand to stop him.

"I carried her back to her room. So, save it."

He smirks.

"You, too?"

"No."

"You sure about that, G.?"

I growl, even though I wonder about myself.

He chuckles and turns to peer through the window into the OR.

"Silver in the mouth? Really, Colin?"

We turn as Dolph strides up. He shakes his head.

I nod.

"Yeah, I already told him. Talking, not mush mouth."

Colin flips us off, and we laugh.

The two enforcers glance at us but don't ask questions.

We haven't told everyone about the she-wolf. Especially since someone rarely comes to the infirmary. Up to now, thanks to Colin's antics. We'd rather limit those aware of her presence until we know more about her. And I damn sure don't want Blaise's guy to see her. My wolf growls at the thought.

If Blaise got his hands on her, I'd do more than silver implants.

But she's safe here. No need to worry.

CHAPTER 15

olph

"Have a what?!"

Colin's brows jump to his hairline as his eyes widen.

I smirk and respond, "A Congratulations on Getting The Casts Removed Dinner. Baby Girl deserves praise for improvement. Plus, we have her cooped up in the infirmary for so long. We'll set it up in the grand hall after the others finish dinner. I'll ask Cook to whip up a special dish."

"Let me guess, a white tablecloth, candles, and flowers?" Garrett asks with arms folded across his chest as he leans against the edge of his desk.

Colin snorts and cocks his head.

"And you expect me to take part in your shenanigans?"

"Yes, and yes," I respond, eyes flicking from one to the other. "The dinner serves another purpose."

"Oh, do enlighten us, Mr. Pussy Whipped," Colin snarks.

I roll my eyes to the heavens, asking the gods for strength and patience to deal with this one. Glancing back at him, I continue.

"She needs to see the three of us behaving as best friends, not snarling at each other's throats. It upsets her. She doesn't want to be the cause of us losing our lifelong friendship."

I pause to look at each of them before I drive home my last point. Garrett remains impassive while Colin quirks his lips. But I capture their attention since neither left the office. I'll take it as a win.

"And the four of us together in a domestic setting exemplifies our future everyday life together as fated mates."

I stop at that mic drop and wait. Let them cogitate on it. The first to speak loses. In three... two... one.

"Like hell!"

Colin jumps to his feet and glares at me. When I return it with a stoic stare, he spins on Garrett.

"You going for this bright idea?!"

Garrett stretches his neck. Tendons pop. Then he shrugs.

"Not a bad idea—"

"Seriously, bro?"

"Listen, she's been through hell, and it's a lot for her to

deal with. She needs encouragement, something positive to keep her moving forward. She may not have her memories. But she should realize her future can be happy. And we've only argued in front of her."

He stares pointedly at Colin and continues.

"And you were rude as fuck when you told her you didn't want anything to do with her. You may not want to complete the bond, I'm not, but you won't continue to be nasty. Especially if she decides to stay with the pack and Dolph claims her. As Alpha, I will not allow disrespectful behavior. Understood?"

And just like that, gone is best friend Garrett and Alpha Garrett steps up.

He can fool himself all he wants to. I see past his facade. He damn sure wants Baby Girl and not just for the sex. His face softens whenever he's around her. Mr. Grump morphs into Mr. Gentle. He'll give in soon enough, and this dinner will be the catalyst.

Perhaps even for Colin.

"Yes, Alpha," he responds, albeit begrudgingly.

Or maybe not.

He'll see the truth soon enough. The gods wouldn't have chosen her for the three of us if we couldn't make the foursome work harmoniously. And we will make it work for Baby Girl's sake, as Garrett said.

"Well, that's settled. We'll meet her in the infirmary at seven to escort her to the grand hall. I'm headed to the kitchen," I say and stride from the office.

"Wuss," Colin calls out.

"Yeah, yeah, yeah. Whatever you say. Let's bet how long you'll stick with the tough guy act. I give it a week max," I throw over my shoulder with a smirk then pause at the door. "What about you, Garrett? What's your number? A few days?"

He chuckles and scrubs a hand over his face.

"I already made my decision, lover boy. While you're with Cook, I'll get her some fresh clothes. Colin will get her flowers," he says with a grin and claps him on the back as he heads for the door.

"Oh, yeah, let me run right into this godsforsaken, never-ending blizzard and dig through a mountain of snow for flowers."

Garrett and I exchange glances then bust out laughing.

Colin grumbles and pushes past us into the hallway, flipping us the bird.

I wait for Garrett to lock the door.

"What? There's more?" He asks as he places a palm on the plate to engage the mechanism.

"What are your plans once this blizzard finally lets up? It can't last much longer."

He shakes his head and walks down the hallway.

"No, it can't, and we'll need to be ready to get out of here for Moen Island. Get communication back. Check on the pack. Clear the roads and helipad. And most of all, find Blaise. If his guy doesn't talk before we're ready, we'll take his laptops and leave him in the dungeons with a team. Have Thyra put her super hacker skills to the test."

I nod.

Since our guy here couldn't crack them with our systems down, Garrett's younger sister can do it. She's a badass hacker wiz who handles technology for the pack and for the company. Garrett keeps her separate from the missions.

"I take it you're really wanting out of here if you're involving Thyra?"

"Yeah, I can't be in both places and want the laptops with me. I need someone here and on the island to communicate in case we need info from Blaise's techie about files and whatnot. Plus, Thyra may be able to find something on Princess."

We reach the turnoff for the wings to the kitchen and to the supply rooms. Garrett heads for the clothes while I go speak with Cook. He offers to make salads and steaks with baked potatoes. I thank him and leave.

Since we maintain the basics at The Fortress, I didn't expect a gourmet seven-course dinner. However, when we return to the city, we'll take Baby Girl to Per Se for a three Michelin star feast.

I spend the next few hours training and making rounds. A glance out the windows from the third floor reveals snow, snow, and more snow. Are the gods determined to keep us here until the three of us claim our mate to what? If so, I'll hunker down for another week to make Baby Girl ours.

With a grin, I head to my rooms for a shower and a change of clothes. Not a bespoke suit I'd wear for a dinner date. That will happen soon enough. And I cannot wait.

"HEY."

I glance up from the pad to find Garrett. Once again, he stands at the foot of my bed with a bundle of clothes. My cheeks flush at the memory of his last visit. But I feel cheeky and grin.

"No panties and bra, huh?"

He smirks and shakes his head.

"Behave, Princess," he responds, as he places the bundle on the bed. "We have a surprise for you. Be ready at seven."

Before I can ask any questions, he strides from the room.

Despite not knowing what's coming, excitement courses through me. I give a whoop and a fist pump. Hopefully, I'll get to see beyond the infirmary and the hallway. Without windows, I have no clue what's happening outside. Sure, we can't go out in the blizzard. But a change in scenery would give my mental state a much-needed boost.

An hour before my surprise engagement, I shower and dress. Instead of wearing the black Henley buttoned up and tucked into the black cargo pants, I open the top buttons and knot the hem at my lower back. From the front, the soft cotton stretches over my full breasts tipped with pebbled nipples and bares the skin beneath my belly button. The pants slung low on my waist held in place by the black belt above my hips. With the black combat boots, I channel a sexy badass.

I brush my hair until it gleams like polished ebony and leave it to hang in a silky curtain to the top curve of my butt. I nibble on my lips to pinken them. Unfortunately, there's nothing I can do about the remnants of the bruises. But I blow a kiss at my reflection and sashay from the bathroom.

A wolf whistle greets me.

My head snaps up to find the trio at the door to my room. I add an extra sway to my hips and toss my hair. A sultry smile lifts the corners of my mouth.

"Hello, fellas," I say in a smokey voice. "I hope I didn't keep you waiting long."

Their jaws unhinge—even Colin's. His amber eyes darken as they sweep over me and pause at my breasts. The nipples tighten to painful points under his scorching gaze. Mine slides to Garrett when he clears his throat as he shifts on his feet. My eyes drop to his crotch. Immediately, my pussy clenches at the burgeoning erection clearly outlined in his pants. My tongue darts out to moisten my lips.

"We've waited forever for you, Baby Girl. A few minutes matter little," Dolph rasps.

I swing my gaze to him.

His topaz eyes glow with an intensity that touches my very soul. There's no mistaken his attraction to me. And I must admit mine to him.

For tonight, I'm going to let myself go of my search for

the past and focus on what my future may hold. And right now, it's these three sexy as sin men. I focus on each one in turn.

The grumpy Alpha whose glacial eyes pierce my soul.

The comforting beta whose musky masculine scent makes me shiver.

The alphahole enforcer whose snark is as good as his bite.

"Well, then, I'm ready for my surprise."

I strut towards them, and they part to let me through the door. With a glance over my shoulder, I hold my arms out to the sides. My smile widens as Dolph and Garrett rush forward. They flank me and loop my arms through theirs, bent at the elbows. I wink at Colin.

"You lead the way."

He smirks and strides around us.

My eyes zoom in on his perfect ass as he swaggers ahead. The powerful muscles flex beneath his dark denim jeans. I think back to a dream during which my fingernails dug into each cheek as he thrust his cock so deep into my pussy, his piercing stroked every wall. My eyes flutter as I bite back a moan.

As though sensing my thoughts, he returns my wink over his shoulder. Tawny eyes sparkle with arrogance. *Gah!* This man drives me out of my mind.

We continue through the various hallways. Garrett and Dolph explain the history of The Fortress and point to various rooms. Some sections are modern, like the hospital. While others, they explain, are part of the original structure built thousands of years ago. The entire structure impresses me as I gawk and ask questions.

When we arrive at a pair of heavy wooden and wrought-iron doors, Colin pauses.

"*Princess*, your surprise."

With a dramatic flourish, he pulls the ornate foot-long handles.

I gasp and my eyes widen, truly surprised.

The doors open to an immense grand hall, austere in design. A multi-beamed high ceiling with wrought-iron chandeliers lit by thick cream-colored candles; cobblestone floors; brick walls; lighting that resembles flickering torches in brackets on the walls and in metal stands scattered around the room. Rectangular wooden tables and chairs line the walls.

In the center of one wall stands an ornate stone hearth with an elaborate stone-carved overmantel. The fireplace is large enough to walk in and stand inside. But tonight, a roaring fire fills the wrought-iron grate, bathing the expansive, grand hall in heat and light.

My gaze settles on a table across from the hearth. More candles in wrought-iron candelabras cast light on the antique dark wood surface. Glasses filled with red wine and water sparkle in the soft glow. White dishes, napkins, and silver cutlery make up the four place settings. Silver cloches cover platters in the center. Between the candelabras, wine bottles rest on silver coasters. A romantic dinner. My heart soars.

Garrett places a hand at the small of my back and

guides me to a chair at the head of the table. He pulls it out, and I smile up at him as I sit. He scoots it forward and strides to the opposite end to sit. Dolph sits to my right and Colin to my left.

"This is amazing. Thank you," I say as I glance from one to the other. "I feel like a queen."

Garrett coughs violently. But he waves off our concern. He grasps his wine glass and raises it.

"Princess, we celebrate the removal of your casts and your bravery. Cheers."

The rest of us raise our glasses. Dolph and Colin add their cheers, and I thank them.

"The food smells delicious," I say as my stomach rumbles. I giggle. "Right on time too!"

"Yes, let's get your plate loaded," Dolph chuckles.

He removes the cloches and adds mouth-watering steak and sides to my plate. Once everyone has their food, we dig in. The conversation flows with their tales of The Fortress and their pack's home on Moen Island. They share their travels all over the globe so vividly, I feel as though I were on remote white-sand beaches or in sprawling cities. Even Colin chimes in.

After we finish dinner, he turns to me.

"I apologize for my rude behavior. It was wrong of me to take my shock out on you. I don't believe in fated mates, so I never expected to meet mine."

My heart skips a beat. He admits to feelings for me?

"Hold on, *Princess*. I still don't want a mate. So, you'll

have to be happy with Dolph. He's not as phenomenal as me—"

Garrett growls, and Colin chuckles, raising his hands palms out in surrender.

"But he'll live to please you, which may help make up for our differences," he says with a smirk.

His words deflate my little bubble. But I hide it as best as I can with a swig of my wine and a nod.

Dolph clears his throat, and I glance his way.

"Do you have any questions for us, Baby Girl?"

I twirl my glass by the stem as I consider his question. The most obvious thing pops into my mind.

"Show me your wolves."

CHAPTER 16

Signy

THEY GAPE at my unexpected demand.

"Colin was so kind as to show me his wolf. Now, I want to see all three of you."

I push back from the table and turn my chair to the center of the room. As I sit, I arch an eyebrow.

"You want me to know about you. Well, that includes your wolves. Show me what you got, fellas."

They exchange glances and communicate silently. Garrett rises and strides around the table to stand a few feet in front of me. Dolph and Colin flank him. Without their eyes leaving mine, they grab the necks of their shirts and yank them overhead. Muscles ripple beneath bronzed skin adorned with intricate tattoos.

The shirts drop to the floor. They crouch and remove their combat boots. As one, they rise to their full towering heights and unbutton their jeans.

I pant at the sight of the V cuts bracketing eight-pack abs and feathery hairs of their happy trails. I want to glide the flat of my tongue along the sculpted muscles and soft hairs to follow where they lead below the waistbands.

My breath catches as the sounds of their zippers fill the room. I lean forward in anticipation of the hidden treasures. And they do not disappoint.

Commando.

Butt. Ass. Naked.

Oh. Oh. Oh.

My eyes bug from my head at their long, thick cocks point directly at me. Pre-cum collects at their bulbous tips. Veins pulse with blood to increase their girth and length. But it's Colin's dick that tops all. Shiny balls appear lodged in the slit and behind the head. They gleam in the candlelight.

I gasp when he fists the base of his cock and tugs. The balls dance. Pre-cum oozes on his fingers.

He chuckles.

"Wolves, Naughty Girl. You want to see our wolves, not our dicks. Although they are magnificent. Right?"

"Y—Yes."

Electricity charges the air in the vast grand hall. It sizzles over my skin and jolts my heart. The crackling of bones reshaping and muscles lengthening join the erotic current. They drop to their hands and knees with eyes locked on mine. I watch, mesmerized. Flashes brighten the space. I blink, then open my eyes at the sound of tapping on cobblestone.

Three immense, powerful wolves prowl before me. Claws on their giant paws strike the floor with each restless step. Their massive heads swivel towards their prey as eyes spark electric blue and golden. Carnal hunger emanates from them.

The waves crash over me, seep into every pore, and fill my pussy with need. It gushes its own greed and soaks my pants. I gasp at the intensity of my reaction to the men shifted into wolves.

Here they are. The three wolves who dominate my erotic dreams night after night. The ones that ignite unnatural cravings in me. Sinful desires.

Then, as now, their growls and rumbles don't evoke fear in me. No. Instead, my body tingles with red-hot sparks. I press my thighs together and whimper with need.

Dolph's golden wolf stops before me while Garrett's jet black wolf circles the chair, eyes on me. I glance left and find Colin's tawny beast just out of reach watching me with molten gold eyes. A shiver races down my spine.

Pressure at the apex of my thighs startles me. My head swings around. The golden wolf nudges me with his snout. Hot breath fans across my lap as he burrows deeper. I gasp as my pussy spasms. He snorts the air then rumbles as he scents my arousal. The memory of Dolph eating me out jumps to the forefront of my mind. I moan as my thighs spread. The wolf rumbles deep in his broad chest.

The hair at my nape moves as hot breath blows across my neck. Eyes close on a moan and loll my head to the side. My hair falls away from my neck. The jet black wolf rumbles at the better access. He drags his nose along the column and up to my ear. He blows against its delicate shell. Goose bumps form on my skin. He nips his way to the juncture with my shoulder. His sharp canines drag across the sensitive area. My body shudders on a guttural moan. His rumble deepens.

A whine draws my attention to the tawny wolf. My eyes open on him. He sits rigidly on his haunches. As our eyes connect, he leans forward, then jerks back. I beckon to him, and he stands with effort. But his head shakes, and he drops to a crouch. His internal battle with Colin prevents him from coming to me. As though I sense the wolf's pain, my heart clenches and I cry out.

Flashes blind me.

"What's wrong, Princess?"

"What hurts, Baby Girl?"

Overwhelmed by it all, my hands fly to my face. I hide behind them, not wanting the three of them to see the roiling emotions that threaten to undo me. One minute, I'm a sexy badass ready for action, the next the pain of rejection strips me bare. I shake my head at their questions.

Then Colin clears his throat, and I lower my hands.

"I showed you my wolf, as requested. I'm glad you liked your surprise. Now, I'll leave you to enjoy your night."

I watch, flabbergasted, as he crouches to gather his clothes and boots then marches away. My eyes squeeze shut to stop the flow of tears. How could this go so wrong in minutes?

Rumbling vibrates around me. Hands rub my outer thighs and knead my shoulders. The audible and physical caresses ease the ache. I keep my eyes closed and allow them to soothe me.

Moments later, I'm scooped from the chair. Dolph carries me to a table and lays me out like a platter. Wordlessly, he and Garrett remove my clothes. Dolph tugs the boots and drops them to the floor while Garrett grips the hem of my Henley. Still knotted, it drags up my torso as I rise with arms extended overhead. My breasts tumble free. They growl in unison then latch onto beaded nipples.

They furl tighter in their warm, wet mouths. Tongues wrap around the sensitive tips and suckle. Teeth nibble and scrape. My back arches as my fingernails scour the wooden surface, seeking purchase behind me.

Hands unbuckle my belt, and my pants rip open as they feast on my breasts. Garrett trails open-mouthed kisses from my breast, along my flank, and down my hip as he lowers the pants. He tosses them over his shoulder and grabs my ankles, yanking me to the edge of the table. Our gazes connect. His feral. Mine wanton.

He licks his lips and lowers his mouth to my throbbing pussy. I cum just from the swipe of his tongue from my puckered hole, over my dripping folds to my swollen clit. A garble cry pours from my mouth as my entire body convulses. He growls and laps as the juices flow from my quivering pussy.

Another growl sounds behind me.

My head whips in its direction.

Dolph squats stroking his ginormous cock. The tip weeps. He smirks as I lick my lips. Grabbing a fist full of my hair in his other hand, he pulls me flat on the table. My head tilts back to a glorious, up-close view. I only have seconds to admire it before he flips around and kneels on either side of my arms. His cock bobs above my face. My eyes fly to his. The smirk widens as he taps his tip against my bottom lip.

My mouth falls open of its own accord.

As he presses it into my willing mouth, Garrett's tongue spears into my pussy. I moan around Dolph's girth. Both men groan in satisfaction.

Garrett licks, bites, and kisses my pussy as he devours it grunting during his feast. My hips circle, grinding on his face. Fingers join in probing my inner walls. One strokes my G-spot, and I keen arcing from the table.

Dolph has none of it.

He fists his cock, sliding it back into my slack mouth. I watch him with hooded eyes as my lips wrap around the slick, bulbous head. My tongue slides along the underside, pressing his cock to the roof of my mouth. I inhale through my nose, sucking him deeper. His girth still makes me gag. Fingernails dig into his muscular thighs. He withdraws slowly, dragging his cock along my tongue.

"Breathe, Baby Girl, and swallow me down your throat. I want to see it stretched by my dick."

I shiver at his dirty words. But eagerly comply to please

him. My throat relaxes as I breathe. He slides deeper, a golden gaze locked on where his cock disappears between my lips. The salty taste of his pre-cum makes my mouth water for more. As I inhale, his musky scent fills me. I need more.

One hand cups his sac and massages his heavy balls while the other hand grips his ass, pulling him closer. His head drops back with a guttural growl. My lips kiss his groin. I hum pleased with myself.

"Fuck, Baby Girl. You take my cock so well," he rasps as his fingers trace the outline of his cock in my throat. His cock twitches, and he groans. "So. Fucking. Good."

Each word punctuated with a rotation of his narrow hips as his hand tightens its hold on my hair. My scalp tingles.

But not as much as my pussy.

Garrett kneels behind Dolph. Electric blue eyes stare at me from over his shoulder. His lips and chin shine, coated with my pussy juices. He lifts my legs straight up and rests them against his chest. They're wedged between him and Dolph's back.

"You are delicious, Princess. But I want to feel you cum from my cock," Garrett growls.

I feel the thickness of his cock as he rubs it along my soaked seam. I mewl around Dolph's cock. He pulls out and taps my lips as I moan wantonly from Garrett's long, slow strokes. My legs tremble.

He increases his pace, and Dolph slides his dick back into my mouth. They find a rhythm as they seek their release. My cheeks hallow out as Dolph's cock grows impossibly larger. He holds my head still and pistons his hips. His eyes bore into mine as his cock pulsates. Hot ropes of cum shoot straight to my belly. I add more suction to milk him of every drop.

Garrett's fingers dig into my inner thighs as his dick surges against my slippery folds. The wet sounds mingle with his grunts and growls. He lifts my hips from the table, changing the angle. His tip hits my clit with each stroke.

"Get ready to cum with me, Princess," he grinds out through clenched teeth. The tendons in his neck stand out as he strains to match his release with my orgasm. "Cum. Cum for me. Now!"

Dolph's still hard cock falls from my mouth. My fingernails dig crescents into his forearms. The back of my head bangs against the table as the orgasm zings down from my crown and up from my toes to detonate within my core. I wail as Garrett roars with one final thrust.

Copious amounts of his cum jettison from his cock to spray my belly and my breasts.

"Fuck that's hot. The Alpha has marked you," Dolph growls as he smears the creamy jizz into my skin, already wet with sweat.

Garrett collapses forward, bracing his hands on either side of Dolph's knees. His forehead rests on his shoulder. Labored breathing mingles with my whimpers.

I close my eyes as aftershocks rip through me. My empty pussy contracts. My legs lower as Garrett climbs from the table. He stands beside me and scoops some of his seed onto his finger. I watch as he brings the fingers to my mouth. I open it on a moan. Silently, he feeds it to me. His cobalt blue eyes don't waver from my mouth. My tongue laps at his digits until they're clean.

"Such a good girl, Princess," he murmurs in a raspy voice as he cups my cheek.

I mewl at his praise and close my eyes, pressing into his palm.

Dolph moves to stand beside Garrett.

My eyes open to them towering over me. No longer in the throes of passion, I feel exposed. I lower my eyes and place an arm over my flushed breasts and sit up. Before I can swing my legs around, Dolph puts a hand on my shoulder. I keep my head bowed.

"You have nothing to be ashamed of, Princess," Garrett says as he tips my chin up.

"Not one thing. You're gorgeous. Perfect," Dolph says as he squeezes my shoulder. "This night is for you. A chance to know us in all ways, including the passion that surges amongst us."

"I agree. And don't mind Colin. He missed out," Garrett adds with a smirk. He rubs his thumb over my swollen bottom lip and continues. "Now, it's time for bed."

COLIN

"Get ready to cum with me, Princess. Cum. Cum for me. Now!"

Fuuuck!

I grit my teeth to silence a bellow as my cock jerks in my fist. The jizz soaks my long-sleeved t-shirt as I cum into it bunched around my junk. My knees wobble, weakened by the explosive force as I eavesdrop on their combined moans and growls through the doors cracked open.

Visions of her sexy as all fuck body sprawled out on a table—at least, that's where I would fuck her or against a wall—fill my head. Her long, silky hair wrapped around my fist as I mount her from behind. Deep, hard thrusts pummel her tight pussy as it gushes around my cock. Back arches pushing her luscious tits up where I pinch and tug the nipples to points. Her ass bright red from the spanking I gave her slaps against my groin. The lewd sounds echo around us. Her luscious scent fills my nose.

And she begs me for more.

As in the dreams, Garrett kneels in front of her with his cock in her hungry mouth and Dolph at her side with her hand wrapped around his cock. She derives as much pleasure in us fucking her as she does in our releases. The four of us perform a carnal dance set to the rhythm of our cries of pure rhapsody.

Tremors run through my body as I let out a silent breath. With my forehead on the doorframe, my heartbeat slows and my mind returns to my surroundings. I glance around then sag against the wall when I confirm no one is nearby. Like a voyeur, I refocus on the threesome.

"I agree. And don't mind Colin. He missed out. Now, it's time for bed."

The shuffling of clothes has me diving for mine.

Damn! Time to bust more than a nut.

I grab my clothes and boots then sprint naked down the hallway. Don't want them to spot me and get the wrong idea.

So, yeah, don't mind me at all.

arrett

"ALPHA, the blizzard let up overnight. Now, it's just wind blowing the snow around. But it's clear enough we can plow the main road and check the communications tower to assess damage. It'll take at least half a day. Would you like me to organize teams?"

"Excellent news. Get going with it and radio Dolph. He may have some input. Keep me posted on the progress," I respond to the enforcer on duty.

"Yes, Alpha," he says with a respectful tilt to his head before he leaves my office.

I pull my mobile from my pocket and place it on the

charger plate. I'll need it at full capacity for when I contact the pack on Moen Island.

Fortunately, my parents—Arne and Idonea—returned from their most recent trip abroad before the mission. As do many former Alphas, he and my mother travel extensively to visit other retired leaders around the world. Undoubtedly, he stepped in since I've been unreachable.

Under normal circumstances, Dolph as my beta would step in, followed by Colin as my lead enforcer. Since they're with me, it would fall to my younger brother, Randel. I'm comfortable with them handling my role as Alpha since they would never let power go to their heads and challenge me for it. Especially since it would be a fight to the death unless one yields. I wouldn't want to end any of them. And the gods understand I wouldn't want Vera—Randel's feisty mate—to come after me.

The thought of my brother who's two years younger than me being mated for over a year makes me think of Princess. If I didn't go on dangerous missions and collect enemies, would I complete the mating bond with her? Even if I'd have to share her with Dolph and Colin?

Well, if last night was an indicator of what we could expect, I'd say hell yes. From the moment we picked her up from her room—who knew combat gear could be sexy?—to the mind-blowing sex even without penetration, made me long for more.

The interest in her eyes as we told her about The Fortress and more of our pack's history proves she's willing to learn about us. I admire her resiliency and strength after the crash and trying to move beyond her memory loss. The carefree laughter and easy humor add to her personality.

I believe she would make an excellent Luna to my Alpha.

But we're not there yet.

She needs to learn who she is and what waits for her, even who. My wolf growls at the idea of her with another male. Funny enough, it doesn't bother him we would share our fated mate with Dolph and Colin. Even when we transitioned for her. Our wolves didn't attack one another in possessive rages or for dominance. Interesting.

And from the way Dolph and I pleasured her, I felt no weird vibes being so intimate with him. Not that I'm interested in males. A hard no. No pun. Nor do I don't judge.

Then there's Colin.

The fucker pulled a stunt again. Even though he tried to clear it up. But it's obvious his wolf wants her. He's just being a stubborn bastard. And if he believes Dolph and I didn't scent his release right outside the doors to the grand hall, he's delusional. We didn't miss his musky spunk as we walked by. It was fresh, so he must have hightailed it out of there when he heard us leaving.

I chuckle and shake my head.

"Hey, Garrett, come in."

Dolph's voice comes over the radio on my desk.

"What's up?"

"I'm headed outside with the plow teams. I want to get a look at the area. When I check it out, I'll report back."

"Sounds good. I'm going to make an announcement for everyone to prepare for departure as soon as the road and helipad are clear. Let me know if we can fly with the wind. I plan to take the helicopters to the island."

Dolph takes a moment to respond.

"I'm not so sure she'd like to get in an aircraft so soon after the crash. We could drive."

I consider his suggestion. No way do I want to upset her. She's doing so well.

"Good point. We'll have to check on the highway being clear once our main road opens up. We have no idea how the surrounding area handled the blizzard. I'm so sick of being cooped up in here, I'll use flamethrowers to clear a path."

Dolph laughs, and I join in.

"I'll be right by your side with one," he adds.

We end the conversation, and I make the announcement over the PA system.

Speaking of Princess, she'll need a hooded parka and gloves. I grab my mobile and set off for the supply rooms. Along the way, I talked to enforcers to check in with them personally. We're a close team, and I prefer contact over a disembodied voice through a speaker. They're all ready to get the hell out of here. Me too.

I grab the gear and go to the infirmary. Doc and the nurse are there reviewing supplies. They'll replace items used during our stay. I check in with them then stride into Princess' room. I pause in the doorway.

She doesn't notice me since she's listening to music on

the iPod Dolph gave her. I doubt she heard my announcement past the earbuds. She smiles as she bops her head. The cascade of silky hair sways to the beat only she hears.

As I approach the bed, I hope the music triggers a memory or something. But my thoughts also go to my memory of her sweet pussy last night. I could drink from her honey fount all day and all night. Then her wet pussy lips surrounding my cock as I stroked us to climax makes me hard instantly. I jiggle my thigh to adjust the burgeoning erection. Damn.

The movement catches her eye. She jumps and yanks the earbuds out.

"Hey! You scared me," she exclaims, then arches an eyebrow and continues in a sultry murmur. "You big bad wolf."

Fuck. Me.

We didn't get to talk after we had sex. She was wobbly on her feet and her eyes could barely stay open. I carried her to the room. Dolph and I undressed her then settled her in the bed. Dolph cleaned her with a warm, wet cloth. She mewled in her sleep, spreading her thighs unconsciously at his touch. He grinned like the luckiest male alive. Ever.

I pressed a kiss to her forehead and snuck a quick whiff intoxicated by her scent mingled with mine from my jizz still on her skin.

Dolph was right, I marked her. Any wolf shifter will detect a male on her. Even a shower—as she's taken this morning—doesn't dispel it.

A possessive grin spreads across my face. My wolf howls to proclaim her as ours.

"The 'big bad wolf,' huh?"

She lowers her head and peeks at me from beneath her long eyelashes. Her ice blue eyes darken with desire. Her arousal wafts in the air.

Between the two of us, it's not clear who's more turned on.

I bend over and nuzzle her neck. Inhaling deeply, I groan in the back of my throat.

"You still carry my scent, Princess," I growl against her warm skin.

My tongue licks a trail to her ear. She shudders as I murmur against the delicate shell.

"Perfect."

She mewls as my lips press a kiss to the tender spot behind her ear. Her fingers grip my biceps. I feather kisses along her jaw and brush them over her lips. Tingles spark from the touch. Both of us groan as our bodies respond to the other.

"Hey Garrett, ready for an update?"

Dolph interrupts the moment and reminds me we have work to do. No time for pleasure. At least for now. Once on the island, it's on.

I press my forehead against hers for a moment before I rise.

"Yeah, give me a moment. I'm with Princess."

"Oh, so you're getting all hot and bothered while I freeze my ass off?"

I chuckle as her cheeks redden. I cup one and brush my thumb over the heated skin.

"You made her blush. Apologize."

"Oh, Baby Girl, you realize I'm only teasing. Forgive me?"

I lower the radio towards her.

"Okay. But you owe me a better apology than that," she says as her lips curve in a seductive smile.

Dolph sputters at her unexpected response. I chuckle and grin at her.

"Well, Dolph, you have an order to obey."

"With absolute pleasure."

"I'll radio back in a minute. Stand by."

I click off and turn to her.

"The snow stopped, and we're preparing to leave as soon as our main road clears. We'll check if they plowed the highway. I left a hooded parka and gloves on the chair for you. If there's anything you want to take, pack it. I'll come back when we're ready. More than likely not until much later. Okay?"

Her eyes cloud with worry. But she nods.

"Okay. I'll be ready," she responds, then frowns. "Where are we going? To Moen Island or somewhere to help me with my memory?"

My chest tightens at the idea of separating from her. Unconsciously, I rub the ache with the heel of my hand.

"To the island. I'll reach out to the Wolf Council to ask if a pack reported a missing she-wolf matching your description. There's no way for us to determine where you came from since the plane could have come from anywhere. New York gets a lot of air traffic."

She nods again as her fingers twist the cord from the earbuds. I place a hand over hers and squeeze. She lifts her gaze back to my face.

"Do not worry. We will take care of you, Princess. Okay?"

"Okay," she whispers.

I press a kiss to her forehead and stand.

"I'll be back later. But if you need me—"

"'Press one on the phone to reach' you. I got. I got."

I chuckle at the sass back in her.

"Okay smarty-pants. See you later."

She waves with a sweet smile when I glance over my shoulder at the door. I raise my hand in response and close it behind me.

SIGNY

HOURS LATER, my mind still reels with the news we're leaving soon. I expected the time would come. I just didn't expect to feel a sense of dread at being away from Garrett, Dolph, and even Colin. We've spent so much time together. I don't know how to behave once we're out of this bubble.

Then it hits me.

Do they have girlfriends or she-wolves? What if the

attraction was only because the blizzard forced us together, unable to get away from each other? Will they still want me?

And when I find out who I am, will I want them? What will I do once I have my memory back?

It's too much to think about. I need some fresh air. Clear my head.

I hop from the bed and lace up my boots then shrug into the parka, tucking the gloves in the pockets. Doc and the nurse left a while ago, so the infirmary is empty. I leave it behind and walk along the hallway in the direction the guys took me to the grand hall. They pointed out the front doors to The Fortress. I hurry towards them.

As I round the bend, cold air blows. The doors stand open as people enter and exit. I shiver and pull my hood on. It covers my head completely, perfect for the blustery weather. I pull my gloves on and stride out the doors.

No one pays any attention to me. I blend right in with them as I make my way along a path in the snow and past two gates. I thought the inside was medieval. The outside takes it to a whole other level. I glance around, impressed by the thick stone walls soaring high into the gray sky.

Outside of the imposing walls, an all white landscape goes on as far as I can see. I turn in a slow circle, amazed at the beauty. Snow swirls as the wind picks it up from the ground. It moves across from one snowdrift to the next. Ahead, the shapes of trees covered in glittering snow mark the beginnings of the forest Dolph told me they run through as a pack.

He says it's magical when the moonlight shines between the giant trees. The pack frolics beneath their branches, dancing in and out of the moon's pools of light. They run for hours and hunt. Their howls ring out across the mountain well into the night.

Eager to see the forest covered in snow, my pace quickens. Before we leave, I want to see it for myself. Especially since I may never return. My heart clenches at the thought. I chide myself and hurry on, thankful the path runs parallel to the trees.

I stop at the edge of path and glance over my shoulder. I'm further than I thought from the wall. My footsteps hesitate as I consider returning. But I want just one peek. I step off the path into deeper snow.

A few feet in, the wind blows my hood back and whips my ponytail behind me like a banner. I close my eyes and let my head fall back as I take a deep breath. The crisp, cold air fills my lungs. It clears my head of the thousands of questions and worry. I open my arms wide and spin in a circle, relishing the fresh air. It's freeing.

With a giggle, I stop and open my eyes. I glance around.

Two men dressed in all white emerge from the trees. If I hadn't seen them move, I wouldn't have noticed them. They blend in seamlessly with the snow. Whereas I stand out in my black parka, pants, and boots. Even my gloves are black.

They stop and glance at one another. Then turn back to me. The wind swirling with snow whips my hair into my face and blocks them from my view. I tuck the loosened strands behind my ears and glance back at the men. They're feet from me. Wow, they move fast. We stare at one another.

I raise my hand in greeting since the wind will carry my words away.

They don't wave back but continue walking through the snowdrifts towards me. They create a path in their wake. The deep snow doesn't deter their movements.

Who are they? I haven't met anyone besides Doc and the nurse. And only caught glimpses of the men who dragged the injured one into the infirmary. But they must recognize me because they keep coming towards me with determined steps.

Garrett told me there's no town around for thousands of miles. They own the entire mountain. So these guys must be from his pack.

It's weird since I've only seen everyone inside with all black clothing and boots. I guess they wear white outside to blend in with the snow. Some military thing? I shrug and watch them approach.

CHAPTER 18

 olph

*"O*KAY. *But you owe me a better apology than that."*

Even hours later, Baby Girl's seductive purr rolls over me. I picture her ice blue eyes dilated from lust and her hot little body as we spread it on the table last night. Tantalizing.

It boggles my mind how easily we fell into a threesome. No awkwardness whatsoever. Not even when Garrett kneeled behind me. His grunts and groans filled my ears, along with the wet sounds of his cock gliding along her pussy lips. Then when he blew his load between my thighs onto her body and collapsed against me with her legs pinned between us, it was downright erotic.

But not once did I want to fuck him, or vice versa. Nah. As they say, to each his own. Just not mine.

Baby Girl's pleasure spiked my own. I craved her passionate cries, the way her body convulsed in ecstasy, and her sated post-orgasmic bliss. And damn if she didn't give me one hell of a blowjob. Dayuum!

My heavy balls draw up, and my cock lengthens at the memory.

And then there was Colin. The fucker pretended she didn't affect him, even though his wolf struggled to get closer. He spouted off some nonsense and left. Only for Garrett and me to scent him outside the grand hall.

Not interested my ass. He jerked off listening to us. If he thinks I'm not going to crack on him, he better think again. I can't wait to see him.

When we get back to Moen Island, I going to make him watch me apologize to Baby Girl. If I have to, tie his ass to a chair and tape his eyes open. Let's see if he doesn't blow his load in his pants as I make her cum on my tongue. I'll even bet him how long he'll last.

I chuckle to myself and continue to watch the team-work on the communications tower.

It took more than an hour to shovel snow from the garage doors, where we keep two snowplows and a tractor. I sent the snowplows out for the main and backup road in case one has better access to the highway than the other. On the way to the backup road, a snowplow cleared around the hangar doors and the helipad. Those who don't want to drive to the island can fly.

The tractor headed to the communications tower and shed followed by specialists and me on snowmobiles. It's further away from The Fortress to avoid radiation affecting us. Even as wolf shifters, we take precautions for such matters.

I'm eager to get the system running again. Losing the ability to communicate externally is the worse part about the blizzard. It's still crazy how the sat phones don't even work. I guess the gods really want the four of us detached from the outside world. But it's time to get back to reality.

As much as I don't want Baby Girl to leave us, she deserves to know who she is. I just hope the connection we made proves solid enough to tie her to us. If not, I won't let her go without a fight. I'll challenge any male to the death who thinks he can keep my fated mate from me. She's ours. Period.

But I'll still send a team to check on the jet crash site. They can get a start on that area. Perhaps they'll find something useful.

Until then, we'll get her settled on the island. The question is, where will she stay? Each of us have mansions. We're next door to each other, with Garrett in the middle. I suppose as Alpha and Baby Girl thus becoming Luna, she would stay with him.

My wolf whines. Yeah, I know. I want her closer to us than next door, too.

Well, then, Garrett will have to get a bigger bed. We share her in all ways, including all night access. But if she needs her space, we'll set up one of Garrett's guest suites as her private retreat. She can make it her own. Hell, she can redecorate all our houses, Colin's included.

We'll make certain she has all she wants and more. A new wardrobe, laptop and mobile, a car and driver, anything and everything. We want her comfortable and happy.

Once we're back, we'll help her channel her wolf. Run around the island with the pack. And there's no doubt they'll welcome her as our fated mate. Sure, some may have a say about us being a foursome. But they'll have to get over it. The gods decided.

Our families will help. My mother Revna will be so excited I found my fated mate. My father Birger and younger brother Bo will see her as another member of our family to protect and to care for. Perhaps Idonea will take a break from her travels with Arne and teach Baby Girl how to be a Luna. I'm not so sure if Brandt—Colin's father— will get involved. But she'll have more than enough support.

And most of all, we'll claim her and complete the mate bonding ceremony. Proclaim her ours for all to see. Since Garrett is an Alpha, I'm sure he'll invite the others, and it will be an enormous affair. I envision her in a gown walking to us at the bower. Her eyes bright with love. Our future written all over her face. Her father hands her to us.

But that reminds me she doesn't know who her father is.

Damn.

"Dolph."

I bite back a growl and turn to one of the specialists.

"The diagnostics show a connection lost. We can fix it. But we'll need more time to repair the tower than we expected."

"Do you have all you need on site, or do you need equipment back at The Fortress?"

"We'll know better once we rappel along the tower to check it up close. Two guys are suiting up and will report back in an hour or so."

"Do what you must. We want to get online as soon as possible."

He nods and turns to the monitors.

Not the best news. But at least it will get done.

I step outside of the shed to radio Garrett. Even though it's large enough to hold the tech equipment and four men, I'm tired of being cooped up.

As I pull the radio from my pocket, I glance around. So much snow it's incredible. The boughs of the evergreen trees sag under the weight of the snow. Deciduous trees creak from the snow on their bare branches. They resemble giant ghosts soaring to the cloudy gray sky.

The wind gusts blow through the trees and carry snow from the ground. It swirls about but not as blinding as during the blizzard. The wind is invigorating. Sharp and clean. I close my eyes to enjoy it for a moment.

As wolf shifters, the cold doesn't bother us. Otherwise, the chill would go through my parka. My wolf frolics tempting me to shift and race through the forest. We'd love to have Baby Girl beside us.

Now is not the time, I need to update Garrett.

"Garrett, come in."

Only a second passes before he connects. He must be as eager as I am to get out of here.

"What's the latest?"

Yup, straight to the point.

"A lost connection will delay us at least an hour. Two guys are rappelling along the tower for a visual check. I'll keep you posted."

He sighs before he speaks.

I share his sentiment.

"Okay, thanks."

He ends the connection.

I go back inside the shed and hope we get answers sooner rather than later. I want to get back to Baby Girl.

COLIN

"So, you want to leave Blaise's fucker here with a few enforcers? And then what?"

I ask Garrett as we stand in the hallway in front of the silver-plated doors separating the stairs to the dungeons.

Should wolf shifters escape up the stairs, the silver in the doors will stop them. Plus, a code is necessary to activate the bolts. We take serious precautions to prevent escapes.

It'll be impossible for Blaise's techie to get free, even with minimal enforcers on duty. My concern is why leave him here at all? He has said nothing. For all the shit he's done, let him die. But it's not up to me. Garrett makes the call as pack Alpha and mission commander.

He nods.

"Yes. Six enforcers to rotate duty in pairs and our tech specialist will standby. Thyra will work on the laptops on the island. She'll communicate with our specialist, and he'll work on the techie," he responds then pauses, cocking an eyebrow at me.

"And no, we cannot kill him," he says, and I quirk my mouth. "However, I will put him in one of the sub-dungeons cells and leave him to starve."

I grin and clap him on the shoulder.

"That's what I'm talking about. Slow and painful," I say. In a grave tone, I add, "He and all the others who harm she-wolves and turn human females for breeding deserve even worse punishment. I hope we get them all and make them pay."

Garrett places his hand on my shoulder and nods.

"I'm with you, brother. Let's check once more on this bastard."

He enters the code and slips a protective glove over his hand to open the doors. They shut behind us, and he tucks the glove in the side pocket of his cargo pants. We make our way down the stairs and enter a code into a second set of doors. They open to a monitoring room where two enforcers watch the camera feeds through the dungeons.

"Hello, Alpha," they say as they rise from their seats at the long desk.

Garrett waves for them to sit as he strides towards them.

"How's the prisoner?"

"No recent developments. He sits on the floor and stares into space or sleeps. He ate breakfast."

At this distance, prisoners can't hear conversations. So, Garrett tells them the plan before we go through the final set of doors buzzed open by one of the enforcers. Silence descends as the doors shut. The temperature drops to barely warm.

We pass rows of cells on each side of the corridor. Unlike the original unlit stone walls and floors with metal bars facing the corridor, these cells are all steel with silver bars.

Lights along the corridor ceiling illuminate the cells. Whomever is inside has no choice but to sleep under the glare of the lights. Too damn bad.

We walk to the end of the corridor to the last cell on the left. And as we saw on the monitor, the jerk sits on the floor. His sunken eyes meet ours as we come into view.

Garrett folds his arms over his chest and widens his stance, staring down at him. I do the same and narrow my eyes. He stares back in silence, determined not to talk.

We put him through it beyond the silver implants. He only gets time between sessions to heal, so it'll hurt again. With one meal a day, he's lost weight and the speed of his healing ability diminishes each day. Yet, he hasn't cracked.

"Where is Blaise?"

No answer.

"Where is Bernard?"

He stares in silence.

"Have it your way."

Garrett pivots on his heel and marches away.

I growl at the fucker before I follow.

We don't speak until we're back in the monitor room.

"We won't be back before we leave for the island. Until we leave, radio me if anything changes. After that, contact me via my mobile immediately. I don't want any mishaps," Garrett tells the enforcers.

"Yes, Alpha," they respond.

After the doors at the top of the stairs close behind us, Garrett turns to me.

"I'm going to check on the progress out front. What about you?"

"Do a round of the interior."

"Good. See ya."

"Yup."

We separate, and I take the stairs to the upper level.

I make my way through each floor and go to the next. I take time to speak with the enforcers I come across and confirm their placement for here or returning to the island. Most are just as eager to get out of here as I am.

On the lower levels, I check the passageways and the gym. The last area is the infirmary. I saved it for last in an attempt to delay seeing the she-wolf. It's bad enough I'll be in the SUV with her for over four hours. Not to mention she'll be next door at Garrett's mansion. At least, I guess she'll stay there.

Knowing she'll be so close and my refusal to bond with her drives my wolf nuts. Oh, well. We'll have to live with my decision. Even now, he whines. I ignore him. Once we're back, I'll appease him with a hard run in wolf form. It will have to do.

"Hi, Colin. Did you need something?"

I glance up to find the nurse smiling at me. Her brown eyes twinkle.

"Hi, no, thanks. Making my rounds before we leave. Do you and doc have everything you need?"

"Yes, thanks," she says then goes back to the paperwork in her hand.

I walk past her towards the she-wolf's room. Duty calls for me to check on everyone in the vicinity, her included.

"Are you looking for Jane?"

I stop and turn back to the nurse. My head cocks at her question. A tingle creeps over my skin. Something is amiss. But I shake it off.

"Yes, I want to be sure she's ready to go, too."

"Oh, well, she's not in her room."

"No?" I ask as the tingle returns. "Where is she?"

The nurse must sense my agitation. Her eyes widen.

"I—I don't know. She wasn't here when I came back."

I spin on my heel and race to her room. I hear the nurse behind me.

"She probably went for a walk in the hallways. She likes to do her exercises."

"No! I just checked the entire Fortress and didn't see her."

I reach her room and barge through the door. My eyes scan the space.

She made the bed. The door to the empty bathroom stands open. A bag sits on the chair.

I rush to it. Inside, I find her pad, pen, iPod, extra clothes, and toiletries. Her unique scent fills my nostrils.

"Maybe she went outside when she saw the activity."

I hear the nurse.

It's possible. But why does my chest tighten as the tingles increase? My wolf claws to break free and find her. I rub my chest as I grab my radio from the side pocket of my cargo pants.

"Garrett, Dolph, come in. Now!"

The nurse whimpers at my growl.

I pace as I wait for them to respond.

"What's wrong?"

"Yeah?"

"The she-wolf. Do you have eyes on her? She's not in her room, and I just finished checking the entire Fortress," I shout, my voice increasing.

What the hell? I never panic.

"Do you see her coat and gloves?"

"No! I'm at the tower."

They speak at the same time.

I glance around in case I missed it. But find nothing.

"No, they're not here."

"Colin, meet me at the front doors. Dolph, head back," Garrett barks and disconnects.

"What do you want me to do?" The nurse asks.

"Stay here in case she returns. Radio us if she does," I respond as I run from the room.

My mind races just as hard, wondering where the hell she can be and hoping she's okay. Perhaps she did go outside and is with others now. She may have wanted a break from The Fortress. Yeah, that's it. Nothing to be worried about.

But why does my heart tell me something is very wrong?

I burst into the entry hall. Garrett's head snaps up.

"No one has seen her. I issued the command to lock down, except for those at the communications tower. I have a bad feeling. We need to find her fast. Shift into your wolf, so we can track better," he says, deceptively calm. But his eyes flash electric blue with his wolf close to the surface.

We strip and shift then bound through the doors. We sniff the air to catch her scent. Despite the wind, we detect it. Garrett barks and races through the bailey and past the gates. We're shoulder-to-shoulder whizzing past enforcers headed inside as commanded. They jump aside to avoid us bowling them over.

Dolph's golden wolf bounds over a snowdrift. He barks and joins us.

Since they cleared the road, it's easy to follow her trail.

We pause at a break in the snowdrift off to the side. She moved from the road towards the forest. Why?

We jump into the snow, careful not to disturb the trail she created as she passed through the snow. Then my hackles raise. Garrett growls. Dolph snarls.

Male wolf shifters. Unknown male wolf shifters. Dozens of them.

Their scents mingle with hers.

We run on then pause. Snow tramped down by multiple pairs of boots leads to the tree line. In the distance, a pair of black gloves stick on a branch. They stand out from the stark white snow. We charge towards them and sniff. Their hers. Left as a message. The fuckers took her!

Growls rip from our throats.

We race into the forest following the trail they made in the deep snow. It leads to a clearing. In the center, the trail ends. We approach with caution. Heads swivel as we scan and sniff the area. No fresh scents.

Garrett takes the lead. At the center, we stop and sniff the snow. Nothing. We glance around. But the rest of the clearing lies undisturbed. Where the hell did they disappear?

Only a helicopter could answer the question. It must have hovered while they climbed a rope ladder inside.

Our eyes lift to the sky, hoping to spot it. But in our guts, we know it's long gone. Dolph throws his head back and howls. The mournful cry sends a shudder through me. Garrett barks and bounds back the way we came.

He's not wasting time and runs at top speed. We follow close on his heels.

Garrett

WE BURST through the gates as the enforcers on duty open them. The front doors open, and we bound through skidding on the stone floor. My side hits a stone wall, and I bounce off. Ignoring the pain in my shoulder, I shift.

Enforcers toss my mobile and clothes to me and some to Dolph and Garrett, who also shifted. I snatch on the pants. I don't bother with the Henley and boots as I run to the doors for the dungeon. Nor do I need to tell them to come with me.

Dolph and Colin flank me followed by the enforcers as we run. I curse at the delay in the code and glove then squeeze through the doors before they open fully. My elbow sizzles from the silver as the corner touches the bare skin. I don't flinch.

Past the next door, we burst into the monitor room. The two enforcers jump as I bellow for them to unlock the door and the one for the last cell. I run through the door and down the corridor.

The fucker has the audacity to poke his head out of the cell. His eyes widen to saucers at the sight of me barreling towards him. He ducks back in.

Too late, fucker.

I run inside, grab his throat, and draw my arm back. His head snaps back from the force of my punch. He screams as his nose breaks and blood spurts. I shake him like a rag doll.

"Where. Is. Blaise?!"

His fingers scrabble at my hand.

I punch him in the eye.

He screams as my knuckles crush his skull.

"I. Will. Not. Ask. Again."

He blabbers nonsense as his face turns blue from my grip on his throat. I loosen it and shake him.

"Speak. Up. Or. Die."

He takes a wheezy breath. One eye stares back at me. Then he closes it and hangs limp, still unwilling to speak.

With a roar, my arm pulls back, my claws extend. They rip through his chest. His eye pops open. His jaw drops. I fist his still beating heart and wrench it clear out of his chest. His eye widens as he stares at his heart pumping blood down my bare arm.

I growl and devour his heart as he watches before his body hangs limp. I release my grip on his throat. He drops to the floor in a heap. Blood pours from his gaping chest.

"Get this piece of shit out of here. Toss his ass in the woods for the other predators to finish off," I snarl, heedless of the blood dripping from my arm to the floor.

The enforcers blink in shock. No one has ever seen me so enraged. Not even during missions in hand-to-hand combat. I always maintain complete control.

But. They Took Her.

I growl, and the enforcers hop to it. I turn to Dolph and Colin. Their eyes burn with rage as their faces morph between man and wolf. They too fell off the edge.

I run from the cell. They follow.

In the monitor room, I snatch up a radio.

"Communications Tower, come in. Now!"

A crackling and someone responds.

"Yes, Alpha?"

"Status on external communications."

"The system is coming on line now, Alpha. Hold on," he says, then a ping sounds in the background. "It's up."

"Wrap up and return to the keep."

"Yes, Alpha."

I press the button on the desk to activate the PA system.

"This is your Alpha speaking. Those not on patrol duty report to the grand hall for further instructions imme-diately."

I turn to the two enforcers.

"Clean the mess and join the rest."

"Yes, Alpha."

The other enforcers carry the fucker in a body bag through the room. I growl with narrowed eyes, even though he's long dead. Then follow them out with Dolph and Colin behind me. I run to my office.

We pass those headed to the grand hall. They don't ask why we're headed in the opposite direction or why I have a bloodied arm. The expressions on our faces silence them.

Inside my office, I grab a towel from the bathroom then

rush to the wall safe and remove the techies' laptops. Sitting at my desk, I swipe the blood from my arm before I open them and enter the password our specialist hacked. The systems boot.

"I'm going to kill that motherfucker."

"Not if I get to him first."

I clench my fists, wanting to destroy something else as Dolph and Colin seethe.

The desktops blink on. Instantly, one chimes with an email alert.

Re: Garrett Moen and Jagger Larson

"Motherfucker! What is he bringing Larson into this for?" I snarl and click it.

Dolph and Colin rush behind me and peer at the screens.

"That's an encrypted message," Dolph says, just as an email alert chimes on the other laptop. He clicks it. "Enter this code in the other browser."

A video appears on the screen.

My heart constricts.

CHAPTER 19

THE MEN STOP in front of me. My head tilts back and back
to stare up at them. They're as tall as the trio. But these
men intimidate me.

"Uh, hi. I'm with Garrett, your Alpha. You probably
didn't know I was here since I was in the infirmary..."

My sentence trails off as more men step from behind
the trees. Okay, maybe a couple were on patrol out here.
But this many? I glance behind me. And no trail of theirs
from the main road? Only mine? Where are they coming
from? Better yet, who the hell are they?

I step back. My eyes dart from one to the other. I can't
see more than their eyes with their faces covered by white
ski masks. They glower at me.

The men step forward. Eerily, not one of them says a word.

Panic grips me as they fan out around me. I whip my head around, keeping them in my line of sight. The wind blows hair in my face. I slap it away. The others are closer.

My mouth opens to scream. But a gloved hand slaps over it from behind. The other bands around my waist. I grapple at their grip as he lifts me from my feet. My legs flail as I try to kick him. I glance around wildly.

A man grabs my arms. He snatches my gloves off and binds my wrists. The plastic cuts into my skin. My muffled cry does nothing to deter him. The hand moves from my mouth only for him to place a gag between my teeth.

Seconds later, I'm flung over the man's shoulder. My arms dig into my ribs and my belly through the parka. The hood falls over my head. My chest constricts as I feel like I'm suffocating. The man runs. His movements jostle me, making it worse as his shoulder strikes my arms. I don't want another break after just healing from the last ones.

It's not until I feel dampness at my hairline do I realize I'm crying. The tears slide over my forehead and catch in my hair. I choke on pitiful moans before they slip past the gag.

Why didn't I stay inside? Where are they taking me? Will Garrett, Dolph, hell, even Colin find me?

My stomach roils. I don't want to me without them. Please let them find me.

The sound of a helicopter interrupts my silent plea. The

man runs faster. My arms and ribs seem like they'll snap at any second.

Wind from the helicopter's blades surge around, lifting the snow from the ground. My hood blows about my head. I squeeze my eyes shut to block out the snow. The sound of the blades increases directly above.

The man stops.

"Hold on to my jacket unless you want to fall to your death," he shouts.

His arm clamped to the backs of my legs releases them. As though I weigh nothing, he slings me around the back of his neck to balance on both shoulders.

I cry out and grab fistfuls of his jacket as I teeter precariously. Then we sway. My eyes pop open to find the ground dropping away. Two men hold the tail end of a rope ladder. He's climbing up to the helicopter! With me, like this?!

Fear constricts my heart and lungs. My head swims. But my mind tells me to hold on. I squeeze my eyes shut as my fingers tighten on his jacket. Please!

Within what was probably two minutes, hands pull me into the helicopter. Frozen in fear, I collapse on the floor. My eyes remain closed as I hear more men climb aboard. The door slams shut, and the helicopter rises.

No one talks to me or touches me. But I listen to them. I need to know where they're taking me and who they are.

I don't get those details. They refer to whomever is in charge as Alpha and beta. The men aboard the helicopter describe women and who they're going to fuck when they get back since the mission made them horny. They're not short on details in that regard.

Positions, female parts, dick size, stamina. They get downright explicit. I cringe at their foul words. In my mind, I beg for Garrett, Dolph, and Colin to save me before these men get their hands on me too. I can't imagine what I'd do. But I would fight if given the chance.

The ride continues for about thirty minutes before the helicopter touches down. The blades wind down, and the sounds of boots stomping on the metal floor let me know the men climb out.

I stay perfectly still, even wishing I could disappear. But when a man yanks me by an arm from the floor, he shakes that idea out of me. I cry out and slouch back. But he jerks me forward. My chest crashes into him.

"Stand up, you bitch! Be lucky Alpha doesn't want a mark on you. Otherwise, I'd slap your teeth out. Better for a blowjob, anyway."

He laughs maniacally. His hot breath buffets my face. It reeks of garlic.

Bile rises in my mouth at his lewd threat and his stink breath. Not wanting to draw more of his ire, I scramble behind him to the helicopter door. He pushes me out into the arms of a man. He leers in my face.

"Did I hear she wants to give blowjobs?" He cackles.

The other men join him.

I will myself to not sob and to keep a clear head. I glance around.

We're outdoors in a field surrounded by trees. Cold air

fills my lungs. Snow blankets the area, not as deep as around The Fortress. But enough to cover the ground and the forest. The last rays of the sun paint the sky gold, red, and blue as it dips behind mountains in the distance. It would be a glorious sight if not for the abominable men around me.

Once again, I'm yanked and forced to walk. Ahead, stand a large barn and farmhouse. Lights shine from within the latter. It's there two men take me. The others jog to the barn. Their jests over who can get to the breeders first confuse me.

I figured they were disgusting from their comments on the helicopter. But farm animals? How repulsive. Sadly, I'd rather they focus their attentions on them than on me.

As we approach the farmhouse, I notice it's not well maintained. More gray siding than white paint remains on the exterior. A few windows lack shutters, and those with them hang askew. The roof misses shingles and slopes in places. The porch steps sag and groan beneath our feet. A broken swing rests below a window. The front door squeaks.

I brace myself for what's—or rather, who's—inside. It doesn't take long for my answer.

"Alpha, we're here with Moen's she-wolf," the man digging his fingernails into my arm announces.

The floorboards creak down the hall ahead of us.

I glance left and right for an escape. Stairs to the second floor rise near us. Rooms on either side of the entry have tables and chairs. A few men sit at them. Their eyes rake over me with interest I don't want. I turn away.

"Well, well, well…"

My head snaps up.

A giant of a man saunters down the hallway. He's shorter by a few inches than Garrett, Dolph, and Colin. But he's wider, with legs as thick as tree trunks and arms to match. A white t-shirt spreads across his barrel chest. Dark jeans cover his muscular long legs ending in heavy black boots. His shaved head gleams in the light as he runs a hand over his beard, surveying me with cold gray eyes.

Another man comes from behind him.

Built the same and similarly dressed, they could pass for twins. Except the second man has calculating green eyes. They study me, focusing on my face intently.

I shudder, glancing away.

The first man, I guess as the Alpha, continues in a French accent.

"Moen kept his secret bitch well hidden all this time. Who would have guessed he had a mate? Too bad she's mine now. Or shall I say, ours?"

I gasp and back up. My eyes dart around, frantic to find any means of escape. Whispering between the two men draws my attention back to them. I watch as the second man and possibly the beta pulls out his mobile.

His finger swipes across the screen, then he holds it out to the Alpha. He stares at it and swipes the screen some more. His eyes flick between the mobile and me.

The hairs on the back of my neck rise.

What are they looking at? And what does it have to do with me? Because without a doubt, it involves me in some way. They study me too closely.

Nothing short of a nefarious grin spreads across the Alpha's face. His gray eyes flash silver as he prowls towards me. I flinch at his predatory behavior. But my eyes won't look away from his.

He looms over me and grips my chin between his thumb and his index finger. He squeezes them together. I whimper. His grin widens.

My head turns left and right as he inspects my face. His hot breath blows over my face as he chortles.

"Well, I'll be damned. You're right Bernard," he says without taking his eyes from mine.

"Yes, Alpha," the man snickers in a French accent.

The Alpha grips the back of my neck and yanks me around to face the others who came from out of the rooms to watch the show. He squeezes and tilts my head back. His nose runs along the side of my neck. He inhales deeply.

I close my eyes as my body trembles in fear.

He stands and tightens his grip.

"This here is Signy Larson, Pack Princess of the Miami Wolves Pack. The Alpha Jagger Larson's little sister and daughter of their former Alpha Marcus Larson. Perfect to breed future Alphas. What a prize we have here!"

What?

My mind reels at his announcement of my name and family. Signy… Larson? A brother and my father? Miami?

What was I doing in New York? Oh, no! Did they perish in the crash?

My knees give out.

But the Alpha's vise-like grip prevents me from dropping to the floor. Instead, I choke myself. Gagging, I raise my hands and claw at his.

He roars as I draw blood.

I still at his savage reaction.

He spins me around.

I watch in horror as his arm draws back and his huge palm flies towards my face. Everything slows.

"You bitch!" He snarls as his hand connects with my cheek.

The blow knocks me sideways. My head jerks as my ears ring. Bright spots dance before my eyes. Blood fills my mouth from my teeth biting my cheek and my tongue. Pain radiates in shockwaves.

"Don't you ever put your hands on me!" He roars as he stomps towards me.

As I drop, I raise my hands. But the plastic ties prevent me from catching myself. My shoulder slams into the hardwood floor followed by the side of my head. I hear a sharp crack then nothing more.

~

SIGNY

. . .

My head pulsates.

My tongue is thick, and my cheek burns inside and out. The metallic taste of blood coats my mouth.

A throbbing in my shoulder spreads down my arm that rests at an awkward angle.

My heavy eyelids open slowly. Without moving my head, my eyes scan the surroundings. Torn curtains hang at a window. Faded floral wallpaper peels from the walls. A closed wooden door is opposite me. My eyes focus on the iron footboard, then my ankles handcuffed to the corners. My bare legs stretch to reach them.

I gasp and jerk my head to the side, biting my lower lip from the pain. Handcuffs anchor my wrists to corners of the iron headboard. I glance down at my body. A thin cotton sheet covers me. Beneath it, I'm naked.

What the hell? What happened to me? Where am I?

This isn't my room!

My heart races as my mind works to make sense of the situation. Then excruciating pain pierces my head. Bile erupts from my mouth. It splatters over my shoulder onto the mattress. I choke as visions race through my mind.

"You can't catch us!" Jagger shouts as he runs with Viggo in our backyard. I toddle behind them, wanting to keep up with my older brothers.

"Oh, honey! You look lovely!" My mother, Sigrid, exclaims as I walk down the stairs of our mansion dressed for my prom.

"Good. We're a family. And family comes above all," my sister-in-law Sage tells me.

"We're going down! Brace yourselves!" The pilot shouts, terrified.

"No, fucking way." "Do you smell that?" "She can't be."

"I don't want anything to do with you, anyway."

"The gods brought you to us."

"Fated mates."

"This here is Signy Larson, Pack Princess of the Miami Wolves Pack."

My eyes pop open.

Garrett, Dolph, Colin! My fated mates!

And I'm Signy Larson!

"Yes, you are."

My eyes snap to the voice, not realizing I spoke aloud. The Alpha who orchestrated my kidnapping dwarfs the doorway. A feral grin shows his sharp canines. A lecherous gaze rakes over my body. He stalks towards me.

My ebony black wolf leaps to her paws. The white patch on her back bristles. Her gray eyes flash silver. A menacing growl pours from her mouth as she bares her sharp teeth.

My heart sings at the sight of her. She's been gone for too long.

I curl my lip and snarl as I glare at him. My arms and legs tug at the restraints, ignoring the pinching of my skin. My hands form fists. The claws dig into my palms.

"Who are you?! You know who I am and must know my brothers and mates will come for me. And you!"

"Oh, so you haven't learned your lesson yet? Now you challenge me, little she-wolf? As for who you are and who will come for you and me, they'll never find this place. If you try to escape, I will shoot your knees with silver bullets. I don't need your legs to breed you."

The blood drains from my face.

Breed me? Dear gods, no!

He's like the men who captured Sasha Volkov, now Vang since she mated Dylan after he saved her. With Garrett's help. These must be the secretive missions he, Dolph, and Colin go on and want to protect me from.

Sasha never speaks of what happened other than to say they never touched her sexually. But she witnessed other she-wolves and turned human females forced to have sex with their captors. Then the females crying when the wolf shifters took their pups from them at birth to be sold. Sasha endured physical and mental abuse. Thank the gods she's better now, and they saved the others with her.

Now, I understand the horror they experienced and why Garrett won't claim me. He knows his enemies will use me to get at him. And this Alpha proves Garrett's concern valid. It can't happen.

I call out to Jagger through our telepathic connection, even though I know he can't sense me from this distance. But I have to try something. I can't stay here. And I can't risk being shot either.

I rein my wolf in. She lowers to a crouch with eyes alert, ready to spring forward at my command. When we get the opportunity, I'll let her free. My features settle, and I still.

"Good for you, you rethought whatever nonsense you

had in mind. Females. So damn dumb. Only worth one thing."

He grabs his crotch with a leer then steps to the bed. The nefarious grin back in place.

"But first, we're making a video for your mate and brother. I wish I could be there to see them lose their shit."

A video? No!

Instantly, my heart pounds against my ribs even as my chest tightens and my breathing stutters. Sweat prickles my underarms while heat flushes my body. Nausea roils my belly. My wolf whines and claws beneath my skin, wanting to protect me.

Wide-eyed, I scoot away from him as far as the handcuffs allow, which isn't more than an inch. But it's enough for him to snarl and to raise his hand.

"Do. Not. Move!"

My body stills, not wanting to experience his beefy hand smashing my face again. My cheek pulsates from the thought of it. I lower my eyes in submission. It won't help me if he thinks I'm challenging him again. I will my wolf to recede. She hesitates but lowers to her belly, head raised.

I sense the rage emanating from him in heatwaves. My ears strain for the whoosh of his hand flying through the air. He remains poised, ready to strike. Seconds pass. My heart races. I hear his arm lower to his side and his hand dig into his jeans pocket. My body sags against the mattress as the breath I didn't realize I was holding slips past my lips on a whisper.

"Better. Now, get ready to smile for the camera, bitch," he commands.

My eyes jump to his face. I scan it trying to figure out his intentions. A sex tape? Him beating me? Gods, what???

The floorboards creak by the door.

I crane my neck to see around him for the source of the noise. A whimper escapes my mouth at the sight of his beta striding into the room. He stops at the foot of the bed and leers down at me. His heated eyes burn away the thin cotton sheet. My face pales, feeling exposed and vulnerable.

"Here's my mobile. Start it up where I left off. I want the entire original on it so I can play it over and over again," the Alpha tells him as he hands the device over. "Let me set the scene first."

He turns back to me.

My skin crawls as his calloused fingers drag along my skin raising the sheet below my pussy. I cringe from the unwanted touch. Then he climbs onto the bed. My heart stalls as he kneels between my spread thighs. He grins down at me.

"Don't look so scared. Now, be a good bitch and smile for the camera like I told you."

Despite my earlier decision to remain still, I thrash against the handcuffs.

"No! Get away from me! Don't touch—"

"Silence!" He roars. Split flies from his mouth as his eyes burn with rage.

I scream as he raises his hand. It swooshes through the

air and backslaps me. My head jerks sideways and my bottom lip splits. Blood fills my mouth again. I splutter and whimper. Tears stream down my face.

My wolf growls and leaps to her feet. If she could defeat two giant male wolf shifters on her own, I would let her free. But I can't risk him making good on his threat to shoot me with silver bullets.

I close my eyes on a whimper and pray to the gods.

"That busted lip and those tears will make for a good video," the beta chuckles. "Ready, Alpha?"

"Yeah, start recording. I'll teach Moen to fuck with my business. He'll regret it for life. Unless I kill the son of a bitch!"

I sob as more tears spill past my eyelashes.

arrett

"WELL, well, well, Moen, you thought you had the jump on me with that misfortunate raid of my facility. You owe me for the bitches you stole. Ruined one of my most profitable locations. And you captured my tech guru.

"You think you have access to the most advanced equipment? Think again. You didn't find the tracker I implanted in him. The signal pulsed loud and clear. I found his location—your secret mountain hideaway—right away. Only that damned blizzard kept me from breaching your medieval fortress and taking it down along with you.

"The minute it cleared up, I sent my men to retrieve my guru and to kill as many of you as possible. But guess who we found by surprise? Signy Larson, Miami Wolves Pack Princess. The bitch told them she's your mate, and you had her in the infirmary. What? You fucked her too hard, or did she just break her manicured fingernail?

"Whatever the case, you can keep my tech guy. I've got a greater prize. The daughter of a long line of Alphas and sister to the current one, not to mention your mate and Luna. I figured you'd get a hold of his laptops. So, I decided to send you a captivating video.

"She's in bed, knocked out. Let's go wake her up, shall we? Here's her room. Give me a minute to get her ready for your viewing pleasure."

The video pauses on his deranged laughter.

"Signy Larson? As in Jagger's little sister? Fuck!"

"I'm going to flay then butcher that fucker alive!"

"He. Is. Dead."

Dolph, Colin, and I snarl and rant. Then the video starts again.

"Fuuuck."

"Gods, no."

"Dead."

I roar at the sight of Princess only covered by a sheet spread-eagle with her wrists and ankles handcuffed to an old iron bed. With. Blaise. Between. Her. Thighs.

A red haze descends over my vision. My wolf snarls, snapping his teeth as he races around. Unimaginable rage rips through me. Claws erupt from my fingers. They gouge the wooden desk. My muscles increase. The cargo pants rip from my thicker thighs. The chair creaks beneath the added weight of my partially shifted form.

My eyes never leave the screen. But I hear Dolph and Colin around me.

Dolph roars. Crash! The bookcase splinters as it's thrown against the opposite wall. Books fly. The matching bookcase slams on top of the first one. Dolph throws his head back and bellows.

Bones crackle. Clothing rips. A flash. Claws scrape the stone floor. Colin's wolf snarls and gnashes his teeth. His massive tawny wolf stalks around.

My chest heaves as I watch without hearing a word from Blaise's grinning mouth. I close my eyes to regain control. Princess. No, Signy needs us. We have to find her and destroy Blaise for good.

I take deep, cleansing breaths to calm my wolf and myself. I envision Signy's sweet smile—not the bloody busted lip. Her giggles as she teases me about being a *big bad wolf fill my ears*. And that's what I'll be to save her—my fated mate.

Being stubborn kept me from claiming her. Now, a maniac stole her from me. From Dolph and from Colin. Based on his reaction, it's safe to say he now admits she's our fated mate. And we'll get her back and make her ours. Forever.

I open my eyes and pause the video then raise my head. Dolph and Colin's wolf stop ranting and face me. They pant with heaving chests. I shake my head.

"Enough. We have to focus and save our fated mate," I say and flick my gaze to Colin. "Shift."

Instantly, he stands as a man again. His eyes burn molten gold with his wolf still close to the surface. But he shakes his head to tamp his other half down and folds his arms across his chest.

"What's our first move?"

"Yeah. How are we going to find the fucker?" Dolph asks in a voice ravaged by howls.

I nod at my best friends and fellow mates.

"We'll have Thyra source the email. Our specialist could do it. But this is our mate, and I need someone who's as invested in her as we are to help us find her."

"They can't be far since she's been missing for under two hours, and they already had time for…" Dolph's words cut off as his eyes flick to the laptop.

I glance at the screen. With clear vision, I see it paused on Blaise licking blood from her busted lip as he grins at the camera. His hand around her throat keeps her facing the camera. She stares at it wide-eyed as tears slip down her pale cheeks. Tousled hair frames her face.

My blood boils, and my wolf nearly bursts through.

"What?!" Colin barks as he rounds the desk. He hisses at the sight. "I swear to the almighty gods, I will bite his tongue out and shove it up his ass. If he wants to taste something, he can taste his own shit."

"I'm with you, brother," Dolph grits through his teeth.

"Time is critical. Dolph, go to the grand hall and brief

the enforcers on the situation. I need a team of twenty to stay here in case Blaise tries some shit. Pick ten here and have ten enforcers fly up from the city. The rest prepare to roll out at the call. Then come back here in fifteen minutes."

"Yes, Alpha," he says and runs from my office.

"Colin, I need you to check our weapons and have more sent up with the enforcers. I want every firearm, man-portable surface-to-air missile, grenade, knife. Fuck, bring the whole damn armory. Use a separate helicopter for them. I want whatever we need at hand, ready to engage. Be back in fifteen, too."

"On it, Alpha. I'm raring to blow the fucker and all with him to smithereens."

"Me too, brother."

He pivots and races from the room.

I scrub a hand over my face and blow a breath out. Not wanting to see the paused nightmare on the laptop screen, I carry both of them to the conference table and turn them backwards. Returning to my desk, I grab my mobile.

I have a few calls to make, including to Jagger. He's going to go ballistic.

Ignoring the missed calls alert, I call Thyra. She answers on the first ring.

"About time! Dad, Randel, and I have been trying to reach you. Didn't you listen to our voicemails? Shit's about to go down, G.!"

I straighten in my chair. The grip on my mobile tightens. The metal creaks. What the hell now? But nothing tops my fated mate.

"No. I have shit happening here and need your help. So, unless your news is life threatening, I'll go first. And watch your language, dammit!"

"Man… if things weren't so crazy, I'd—"

"Thyra!"

"Fine! Jagger Larson, Miami Wolves Pack—"

"I'm aware of who he is, and he's next on my call list. Continue."

She huffs and goes on.

"His sister is missing. He told Dad the last location on her private jet was upstate. They couldn't find anything in the area through their research. He asked for Dad's help. When Jagger gave me the coordinates, it's near The Fortress. Please tell me you have her. He's frantic as fuck. And flew up over a week ago. But the blizzard kept him and us from you. Dad gave him permission to stay in Manhattan. He's here with his brother, pack doctor, and Dylan. They flew up by helicopter a while ago. They should've landed at the helipad by now—"

I snap my head up at a commotion outside my office door.

"Hold on, Larson! Alpha will tell you all we know," Dolph shouts. "Wait!"

The door bursts open. It bangs back on its hinges. The doorknob breaks as it hits the stone wall.

Jagger towers in the doorway. He's as massive as me but an inch shorter. His ice blue eyes shoot silver daggers at me. He stalks into the office, eyes locked on mine.

I stand and round my desk.

Ordinarily, I wouldn't tolerate such a display of disrespect of me in my territory. I flick my gaze to Dylan, who enters next. And he should remember what happens when wolf shifters or anyone charge into my office as he did at Moen, Inc. I catch sight of Viggo's fiery coppery red hair over Dylan's shoulder. Last to enter is a male I'm not familiar with. He must be the pack doctor Thyra mentioned.

But these are different circumstances. Jagger and Viggo's sister is missing, and they couldn't reach me near where she was last spotted. If it were Thyra, I'd react the same. Fuck protocol.

"I scent my sister in this fortress mingled with fresh blood, Moen, and no one will tell me where she is. Tell. Me. Now."

His calm tone belies the forceful wave of Alpha command that pushes at me.

I stagger but hold my ground.

"I'll forgive your behavior, Larson, since I understand your reason. But time is critical, and I need to send a message to my sister to hack. Give me one minute, and I will tell you all."

His ice blue eyes—so like his sister and brother—narrow. His Adam's apple bobs as he swallows back a retort. He nods and crosses his arms over his chest, widening his stance.

Viggo and Dylan flank him while the doctor stands behind him.

I nod in acknowledgment of them as Dolph and Colin

enter the office, closing the door behind them. It creaks on its hinges but closes fully. They stand on both sides of my desk. I stride to the laptops and bring the mobile back to my ear.

I angle my body so Larson and the others can't see the screens. Then I tell Thyra I'm sending her an encrypted email with a video file she needs to source, and if she can't, to contact me immediately. I end the call and place the phone in my cargo pants pocket.

"Where the fuck are the rest of your clothes, and why are you pants torn? If you touched my sister without my approval and against her will, I will—"

"Jagger, we have a much larger issue. The private jet crashed in the blizzard, killing all but Princ—I mean Signy. Dolph, Colin, and I, along with some enforcers, found the site. The crash injured her badly—"

"Is. She. Alive?!"

I hold up my hand to ward off his Alpha command, as if that would work, and nod.

"Yes. Our doctor had to put her in a medically induced coma for a week. When she awoke, she didn't know who she was. She has amnesia—"

"Take us to her."

Unconsciously, my eyes flick to the conference room table where the laptops sit facing backwards again. Naturally, Jagger catches the movement. Before I can stop him, he charges over and yanks them around. I can tell when he sees the paused video.

His head snaps back as he inhales sharply. His hands

form fists. He raises them to smash the laptop. But I push him sideways. He growls and whips around.

"Who the fuck is that?!"

Viggo's shout followed by a string of curses fills the room.

I glance back at him standing in front of the laptops. Mistake.

My jaw explodes.

"You let my baby sister get kidnapped while under your protection?!" Jagger's roar rings in my ears as his lethal punch dislocates my jaw.

I drop to one knee as pain radiates across my face and the breath leaves my lungs. My eyes water as I cup my jaw and snap it back into place. Thank the gods for our ability to tolerate pain and for our enhanced healing. A human's skull would have shattered.

I climb to my still bare feet as Dolph and their pack doctor struggle to hold Jagger from attacking me again. He continues to shout. My eyes sweep the room to find Colin in a glaring face-off with Viggo and Dylan.

"Between all of you fuckers, you couldn't protect Signy?!" Viggo shouts.

Colin growls, "Fuck off! Do you think we'd let them take her? She's our fated mate!"

Silence descends.

Jagger stops moving abruptly. His head swivels towards me.

"What the fuck did he just say? Fated mate? Our???"

I spit blood on the stone floor before I can speak.

"Yes. Dolph, Colin, and mine. Signy is our fated mate."

Viggo curses and spins away from Colin. Her brother paces the floor with clenched fists.

Jagger's molars grind loud enough to be heard over his brother.

Dylan and the pack doctor narrow their eyes on us.

"Listen, Jagger and Dylan, you know what it is to know your fated mate. I don't know about you two," I say as I look between Viggo and the pack doctor. They nod. "The only difference is Signy has three—"

"I don't think so, Moen," Jagger growls. He raises his hand when the three of us protest and continues. "But I don't have time to get into it with you now. We have to find my sister. Tell me what happened."

I fill him in up to the last time anyone saw her, being the nurse in the infirmary. I hesitate before I go into who took her. He growls low in his chest. I grip the back of my neck and squeeze. Then continue.

"Dylan, you know the missions we do—"

"Fuck. No." He growls as his sizable hands fist at his sides. He turns to Jagger. "Fucking breeders."

All the air gets sucked out of the office.

Jagger turns flashing silver eyes on me then Dolph and Colin and growls.

"Pray the gods are on your side because if I do not get my baby sister back, I. Will. End. You. All."

THANK you for reading *Signy's Mates*!

Their story continues in *Signy Claimed: A Wolf Shifter Fated Mates Reverse Harem Romance*. If you enjoyed this book, I would so appreciate your review as they make a huge difference for indie authors. Be sure to sign up for my newsletter for latest info about the series, new releases, and a FREE book **bit.ly/CLBooksDylanTheRogue** for Dylan and Sasha's story! Turn the page for a preview of the start to the Billionaire Wolves Series—*Jagger The Temptation: A Wolf Shifter Fated Mates Paranormal Romance.*

PREVIEW JAGGER THE TEMPTATION: A WOLF SHIFTER FATED MATES PARANORMAL ROMANCE

agger

"THE QUARTERLY NUMBERS show an increase in profits. More than projected because of the opening of the beachfront resort in Charleston earlier than planned. The general manager reports the property sold out for the first four months…"

I nod as my Vice President of Hotels and Resorts for Larson Enterprises, Inc. continues his update. My mind focuses partially on his presentation.

For the last few weeks, I can't seem to focus. I don't know whether lack of sleep causes the lapse or something else. Dreams of another dominate my nights. They remain just out of reach, on the fringes. But it's their silent pleas for help that keep me tossing. A vibration from them of fear and sadness draws me closer. My instinct kicks in, and I want to save them, protect them.

Each dream brings me closer to them. But they remain just out of reach. I wake tangled in silk sheets. An arm extended as my hand reaches for them. Last night I called a name. However, as the last vestiges of the dream slipped away, the name dissolved with it.

I growl low in my chest in frustration.

My COO shifts his gaze to me. His wolf senses picked up my displeasure with ease.

I shake my head at Tag Dahl.

He cocks his head at me.

As my best friend, he's known me since we were pups. Born within a few weeks of each other—him to our pack's enforcer and me to our Alpha—Tag knows me as well as I know myself. I haven't mentioned my dreams to him, not that he'd think me nuts. No. I just don't know what they mean and if they warrant a conversation for analysis.

And Tag would delve into their meaning.

As my beta, he's my right-hand man. Anything that involves me and can impact our pack, he wants to solve the puzzle.

But this one will remain under wraps until I figure it out. So, I shake my head again and turn my attention back to the presentation. Even as I will my mind to pay full attention. I remove my personal hat. Then I firmly affix the one for my roles as CEO and Chairman of the Board of the luxury hotels, fine dining, clubs, and lounges company my family founded in Miami.

An hour later, a persistent Tag strides along with me to my suite of offices in The Larson Tower on Biscayne Bay. We pass through the executive floor as staff—wolf shifter and human—acknowledge us. The unaware humans often stare in awe at our formidable sizes. We're both six feet, seven inches of pure muscle and move with predatory grace. We nod in return but continue without pause.

I know Tag wants to find out what's up with me. I'll allow his henpecking since we're so close. Otherwise, I do not tolerate others in my business. No. One.

"Alpha, you have a few voicemails, sir."

"Thanks, Ginny," I respond to my administrative assistant as I open the double doors of my office. "Kindly hold my calls."

"What's up, Jagger?"

I bite back an irritated growl—lack of sleep will have you pissed, even at your best friend who only wants to help.

"You want a drink?" I ask as I unbutton the jacket of my bespoke three-piece Brioni suit and stride to the bar cart. It's after five-thirty, and I can use a stiff one before I head out to Club Sol & Mani for some much-needed sexual relief.

"Sure, thanks."

I take my time pouring two fingers of scotch into the Baccarat crystal tumblers. Absolutely no rush to have Tag pick at my psyche. My ears pick up his almost silent huff, and I chuckle to myself.

"Don't delay this conversation, Jag. You've been off for a few weeks now, and I've given you space," he says, then nods his thanks for the liquor. "What's up with you?"

Again, I allow him to question me, even though I'm his Alpha and my word is final.

I lower myself onto the dove gray tufted leather sofa in the seating area. Tag takes a chair opposite and places an ankle over a knee. I sip my drink as I consider my words. He knows better than to interrupt at this point.

"Dreams."

He cocks his head at the simple one-worded response. I shrug and take another sip.

"For the past few weeks, dreams invade my sleep. Every. Single. Night. Someone's in trouble. But I can't catch their name or where they are to help them," I sigh and stare out the window.

The panoramic view across Biscayne Bay with jet skiers and megayachts on its dazzling surface out to the azure Atlantic Ocean helps to quiet the inner turmoil my wolf and I sense. He turns his massive silvery white head to stare at me with accusatory ice blue eyes. It's as though he knows something I don't and pissed I'm not aware. I run my fingers through my white blond hair as I think on it, then shake my head. No clue.

"What do you recall?" Tag asks as he leans forward and places his elbows on his knees, the scotch tumbler balanced between his sizable hands.

I shrug.

"A brightness in the background prevents a clear view. I know it's outdoors since I hear the hum of insects and feel the warm sun on my skin. Naked skin. So, I must have shifted and returned to my human form."

Another sip of scotch, and I stand to pace my office.

Instinct tells me these are no ordinary dreams. But each morning I account for the whereabouts of my pack, and no one turns up missing. Not knowing who calls for my help drives me and my wolf mad.

I growl and toss back the rest of my scotch. A few long strides and I refill the tumbler.

"No one in our pack seems in trouble. I'll stop by the she-wolves' residences on my way home just to make sure. A few of our unmated males flew to New Orleans for the weekend. I'll shoot a text to them and make sure they didn't get into anything on Bourbon Street."

With a nod of agreement, I hold the decanter up. Tag declines a refill—ever the responsible one. Fine. It's not like wolf shifters can get drunk. Well, not too much. Our systems process substances differently from humans. All the better for us, especially when I'm in this pissy mood.

"Well, you know they say fated mates can have dreams about the other. The more frequent and intense they become, the closer the pair gets to their first encounter," Tag says. His emerald green eyes scan my face for a reaction. He knows I've waited all these years for my fated mate—and will continue to do so.

Despite my father's damn near daily persistence, I issue

the claiming bite and complete the mating bond with a single she-wolf. The last eleven years of nearly nonstop mating runs, with the she-wolves in my pack and those from nearby cities—hell, even overseas. Or galas at our hotels and mixers at our clubs, an accidental encounter, all to persuade me to select a she-wolf as my mate. None of them tempt me in the slightest.

All the she-wolves desire to bond with me. Then the supposed prince—and they were eager to lose their slippers and thongs for me to pick up——now the Alpha of the Miami Wolves Pack. Correction, *Billionaire Wolves of Miami* as the other packs refer to us. With good reason, since we're the most powerful pack in the South.

Several millennia ago, Scandinavian Viking wolf shifters sailed from the Old World and landed along the East Coast of what's now the United States. The six packs headed by best friends who sought new lands moved throughout the continent to form territories with ours settling here. We maintain close ties with our brethren through friendship, mating, and business. Plus, our Ruling Council gatherings keep us informed of happenings throughout the packs.

And even going that far and wide, I have yet to meet my fated mate. However, I will wait for her.

Hell, my wolf demands it as he gets agitated when he senses a she-wolf's burgeoning interest. Sure, he'll sit back while I fuck since it fills a need and doesn't equate to being mated. Wolf shifters—male and female—have strong sexual appetites. We don't have the same hang-ups as humans over casual sex, no sex before marriage, and whatever other bullshit they come up with. It's a part of our lives, just like eating or breathing. A need we won't suppress. Particularly with the built-up tension raging through my body. However, his pacing and snarls have increased recently, too.

So maybe Tag is on to something.

My *fated* mate.

A she-wolf whose scent I was born with teasing my nostrils. When she appears, I will recognize her by her distinct scent. No other will bear her uniqueness. Someday we will meet. I will give her my claiming bite, and we will have our mate bonding ceremony for all the clans to witness. I will make her mine forever.

The thought she may be in trouble makes my blood boil and my wolf snap his teeth, ears flat to his head. Our protective instinct on high alert.

So, I won't give up on finding my fated mate—or on us. No matter how many times my father bugs me about the need to bond with another. I'm no longer the teen who had to obey.

I am Alpha now.

"We're here, Alpha."

I glance up from my mobile screen and out the tinted window.

So focused on business emails, I didn't notice my driver

pull my Black Badge Rolls-Royce Cullinan into the driveway for Club Sol & Mani Miami. The flagship of six exclusive, luxury, members only BDSM clubs Larson Enterprises owns sits on Ocean Drive directly across from the Atlantic Ocean in a South Beach historic, beachfront gated mansion.

"Great, thank you, Cole," I respond. "I'll take it from here and will text when I'm ready to go home."

"Yes, Alpha. I'll get the door for you."

I wave him off and reach for the handle, only for the club's valet to open the door. A nod to Cole and a thanks in the form of a hundred to the young wolf shifter, and I stride to the scrolled wrought-iron and glass doors of the Spanish-style mansion. Laughter from members as they frolic in the mosaic-tiled pool within the sun-filled court-yard floats in the balmy evening air.

"Good evening, Alpha," the doorman says with a respectful bow of his head. I shake his hand and palm off another hundred. He thanks me as I move on.

"Hello, Alpha!" The two she-wolf greeters chorus cheerfully as I walk through the opulent lobby to the elevators. Another two C-notes and I'm on the elevator headed to my personal suite.

Tonight, I'll play in privacy rather than amongst other members in Exhibition where demonstrations and performance rooms provide entertainment—or inspiration. Nor will the Dungeon do, despite my affinity for the spacious section devoted to public forms of BDSM play. Those not in the lifestyle may think it's a medieval dungeon for torture with the St. Andrew's Crosses, spanking benches, chains suspended from the ceiling, and more. To me, the pieces and assorted whips, floggers, canes, and implements are only to be expected.

The soft thrum of sensual music greets me as I step out of the elevator and into the hallway. The rhythm vibrates through my core as intended to amp arousal for what lies behind the closed doors of the eight private suites. Members can reserve them in advance should they prefer the same privacy I wish for tonight.

Each suite decorated by theme has various BDSM pieces, implements, and toys. A nice variety of options to choose from. However, my suite remains for my personal use only.

I press my palm against the plate by the door of the corner suite, and the locks disengage.

"Good evening, Alpha."

My head jerks up. What the fuck?! I allow no one in my space without my consent. My ice blue eyes adjust to the candlelit room. On my custom-built mahogany wood, king-size bed cornered by four thick carved posters and a brass lattice canopy with rings strategically attached sits a she-wolf from my pack. And not just any she-wolf. The sable-haired hellion.

"Melissa, what the fuck are you doing in my suite?!" I snarl as I stalk towards her.

She jerks back as though slapped but recovers quickly. Fully naked, she rises from the bed with the prowess of a wolf in hunt mode and slinks towards me. Amber eyes glow in the candlelight. She tosses her waist-length sable brown hair over her shoulders. Her sleek figure with high perky tits tipped by puckered rosy nipples, flat belly, narrow waist, slim hips, and long, toned legs would make any male salivate.

Not me.

Even though I planned to fuck her tonight—after I *invited* her to my suite—my stomach churns at the thought as my wolf growls low in his broad chest. He's not happy, nor am I.

Melissa is one of my regular sexual partners. We scratch the itch for each other from time to time. However, it's not like we're exclusive. Many a she-wolf join me for carnal pleasures. As Melissa has with other males. And I've made it clear I am not interested in bonding with her.

But after this stunt, this may very well be the last time I hookup with her. If she thinks she can enter my domain uninvited, she's confused. And I will speak with the club manager about her gaining unapproved access.

I have no intention of giving Melissa any ideas.

Not happening.

For one, Melissa thinks she's the alpha since the other male wolf shifters in our pack bow down to her beauty and succumb to her whims. I won't have it.

Not to mention she's a bully. Another trait I will not tolerate. I treat everyone in our pack with respect. They may not be my equal, but I don't make them feel less than.

And the most important reason... She's not my fated

mate. The only wolf shifter who will enter my domain as she pleases.

My wolf agrees with a flick of his feathery tail.

"Melissa, I have told you we fuck. Nothing more"—I raise my hand to stop her response—"You have no right to enter my personal suite without my permission. None. Get dressed. I will inform the club manager not to allow you entry ever again. This is it. Do you understand?"

She blinks, then her mouth opens.

I fold my arms over my chest and stand with feet spread far apart in a dominant manner as I pin her with an arctic gaze.

Naturally, Melissa glares back and mimics my stance as her eyes blaze golden fire.

"Jag—"

"Alpha! Alpha, Melissa. And do not forget it. We may have fucked. But you will respect me as your Alpha. Get. Dressed. And. Go. Now."

She lifts her chin in defiance, then reconsiders when I slap my sizable palm on my muscular thigh. Her eyes widen at the warning. Then she scurries to the chair and gathers her clothes to her flushed chest.

"Yes, Alpha!" She exclaims.

With a stern eye, I watch as she dresses quickly.

Melissa stops at the door and glances at me over her shoulder. Her oval-shaped face pinched with worry. She knows she took it too far this time.

"Sorry, Alpha," she whispers, then opens the door and leaves.

I sigh and sink onto the bed.

Well, there goes the idea of releasing tension. More just built up.

With his tongue hanging out from the side of his mouth, my wolf yips. Ice blue eyes gleam with mirth. It's as though he laughs at my misfortune.

I growl at him and slump back on the navy blue silk pillows. My thoughts drift to my conversation with Tag. Perhaps fate doesn't want me with another since my mate will appear soon. My eyes close on a sigh.

Where are you?

~

Click the Image Below or Visit books2read.com/u/ mZEL2e For Your Copy

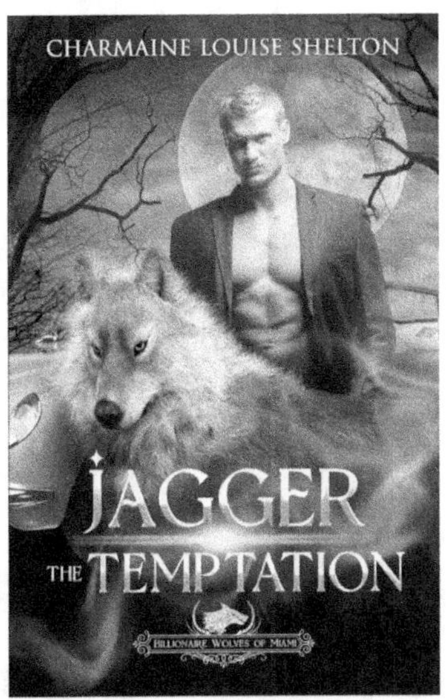

Jagger The Temptation: A Wolf Shifter Fated Mates
Paranormal Romance

NEXT IN SERIES SIGNY CLAIMED: A WOLF SHIFTER FATED MATES REVERSE HAREM ROMANCE

How far will my wolf shifter fated mates go to claim me? They'll burn down the world and take down anyone who stands in their way. Including me.

GARRETT THE GRUMPY leader whose glacial eyes pierce my soul.

Dolph the comforting beta whose musky masculine scent makes me shiver.

Colin the brute enforcer whose snark is as good as his bite.

THEY REALIZE I'm their fated mate and want me as their queen of the New York Wolves Pack.

. . .

BEFORE I RECOVER MY MEMORY, I'm snatched from The Fortress. Now, their enemy holds me, and they will do anything to get me back. But what do I want, or does it matter?

THEIR SPICY REVERSE harem paranormal romance is a standalone trilogy in the sizzling Billionaire Wolves Series of interconnecting stories featuring wolf shifter fated mates romance. Get a glimpse of their dynamism in other books.

~

Click the Image Below or Visit books2read.com/u/ 4j5Q5D For Your Copy

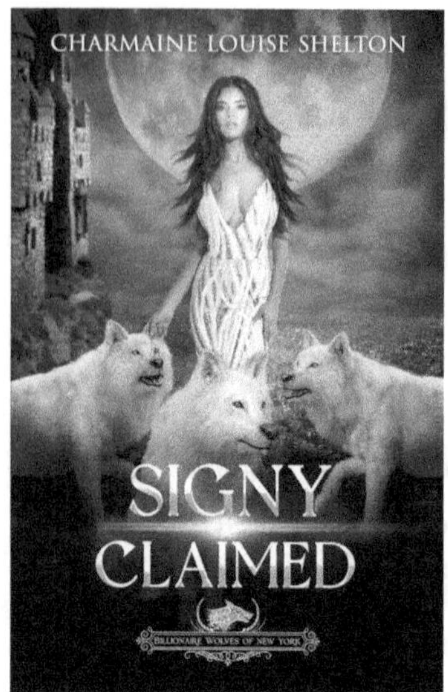

Signy Claimed: A Wolf Shifter Fated Mates Reverse Harem Romance

WANT FREE BOOKS?

Want to know what happened to Jagger's best friend Dylan? Find out in *Dylan The Rogue: A Wolf Shifter Fated Mates Paranormal Romance* your FREE Book!

Click Cover Below or visit **bit.ly/ CLBooksDylanTheRogue** to subscribe to my newsletter for latest news and launches, books from my author friends, and sizzling reads in book promotions. Plus, start reading the steamy fated mates romance for bad boy wolf shifter Dylan.

ALSO BY CHARMAINE LOUISE SHELTON

STEELE INTERNATIONAL, INC.

A BILLIONAIRES ROMANCE SERIES

Discover My Desires Sebastian & Lola Prequel

(Available Exclusively to Subscribers)

Fulfill My Desires Sebastian & Lola Part I

Heighten My Desires Sebastian & Lola Part II

Ignite My Desires Roger & Leonie Part I

Stoke My Desires Roger & Leonie Part II

Justify My Desires Roger & Leonie Part III

Deepen My Desires Sebastian & Lola Part III

Capture My Desires Malcolm & Starr Part I

Embrace My Desires Malcolm & Starr Part II

Cherish My Desires Malcolm & Starr Part III

A Trilogy of Desires Sebastian & Lola Parts I-III

A Trilogy of Desires Roger & Leonie Parts I-III

Series Extras

Series Playlist

STEELE INTERNATIONAL, INC. - JACKSON
CORPORATION

A BILLIONAIRES ROMANCE SERIES CROSSOVER

Tempt My Desires Lachlan & Haley Part I

Tease My Desires Lachlan & Haley Part I

Grant My Desires Lachlan & Haley Part III

JACKSON CORPORATION

A BILLIONAIRES ROMANCE SERIES

Evoke My Desires Laurent & Yessenia Prequel

Light My Desires Laurent & Yessenia Part I

BILLIONAIRE WOLVES SERIES

WOLF SHIFTER FATED MATES PARANORMAL ROMANCE

MIAMI

Jagger The Awakening

(Available Exclusively for a Limited Time in Lunar Rising: A
Collection of Paranormal Romance)

Dylan The Rogue

(Available Exclusively to Subscribers)

Jagger The Temptation

Rust The Rejected

Tag The Redemption

Viggo The Obsession

NEW YORK

Signy's Mates

Signy Claimed

Signy Forever

ABOUT CHARMAINE LOUISE SHELTON

Charmaine Louise Shelton loves a dominant Alpha hero—human, shifter, or vampire—as long as he's a billionaire and sexy as sin! Her romance novels take readers into the heroes' glitzy, glamorous, steamy worlds as they chase after independent women who unexpectedly capture their hearts. Want to experience some more? Download a free book at CharmaineLouiseBooks.com!

Find her at:
CharmaineLouiseBooks.com

Follow her on social media on your favorite channels below and **download your Free Book** at CharmaineLouise Books.com.

Fulfill Your Desires.

DEDICATION

To my awesome and dedicated beta readers and ARC Team, my amazing author friends, and this incredible community for their support.

And most of all to you, my loyal readers who love these couples as much as I do.

Thank you!

Fulfill Your Desires.

xoxo
Charmaine Louise Shelton